Lonico

Beyond the Dark Mountain

Lonico

Beyond the Dark Mountain

Graham Angus

mosaic press

Library and Archives Canada Cataloguing in Publication

Angus, Graham F. 1979-
Lonico : beyond the dark mountain / Graham F. Angus.

ISBN 978-0-88962-923-3

I. Title.

PS8601.N486L65 2010   C813'.6   C2010-906365-1

No part of this book may be reproduced or transmitted in any form, by any means, electronic or mechanical, including photocopying and recording, information storage and retrieval systems, without permission in writing from the publisher, except by a reviewer who may quote brief passages in a review.

Published by Mosaic Press, offices and warehouse at 1252 Speers Road, Units 1 and 2, Oakville, Ontario, L6L 5N9, Canada and Mosaic Press, PMB 145, 4500 Witmer Industrial Estates, Niagara Falls, NY, 14305-1386, U.S.A.

Copyright © 2010, Graham F. Angus

Cover illustration by Tessa Angus
Interior illustrations by Diana Hillman
Printed and Bound in Canada.

ISBN 978-0-88962-923-3

Mosaic Press in Canada:
1252 Speers Road, Units 1 & 2
Oakville, Ontario
L6L 5N9
Phone/Fax: 905-825-2130
info@mosaic-press.com   www.mosaic-press.com

Mosaic Press in U.S.A.:
4500 Witmer Industrial Estates
PMB 145, Niagara Falls, NY
14305-1386
info@mosaic-press.com

For my family.

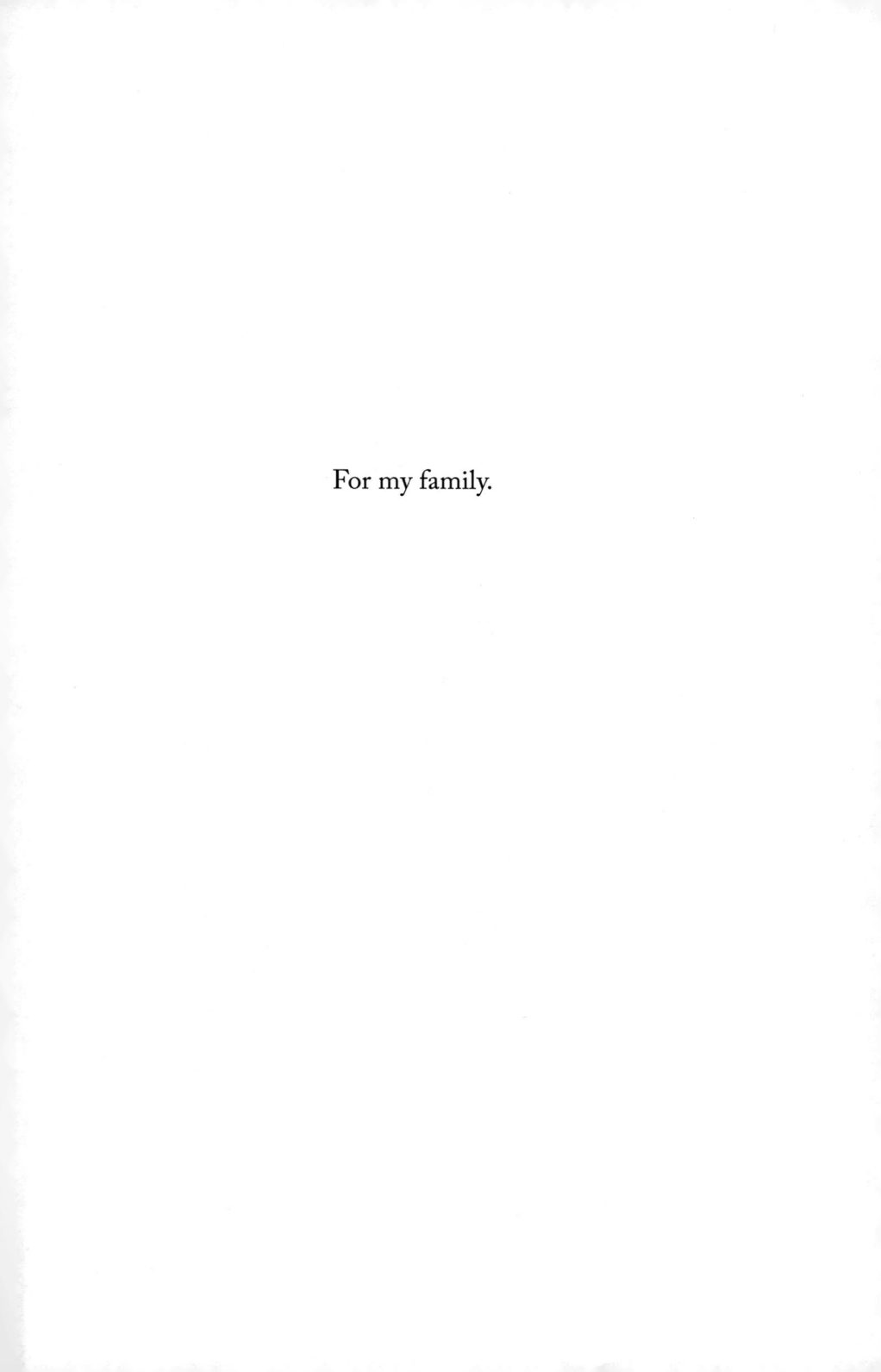

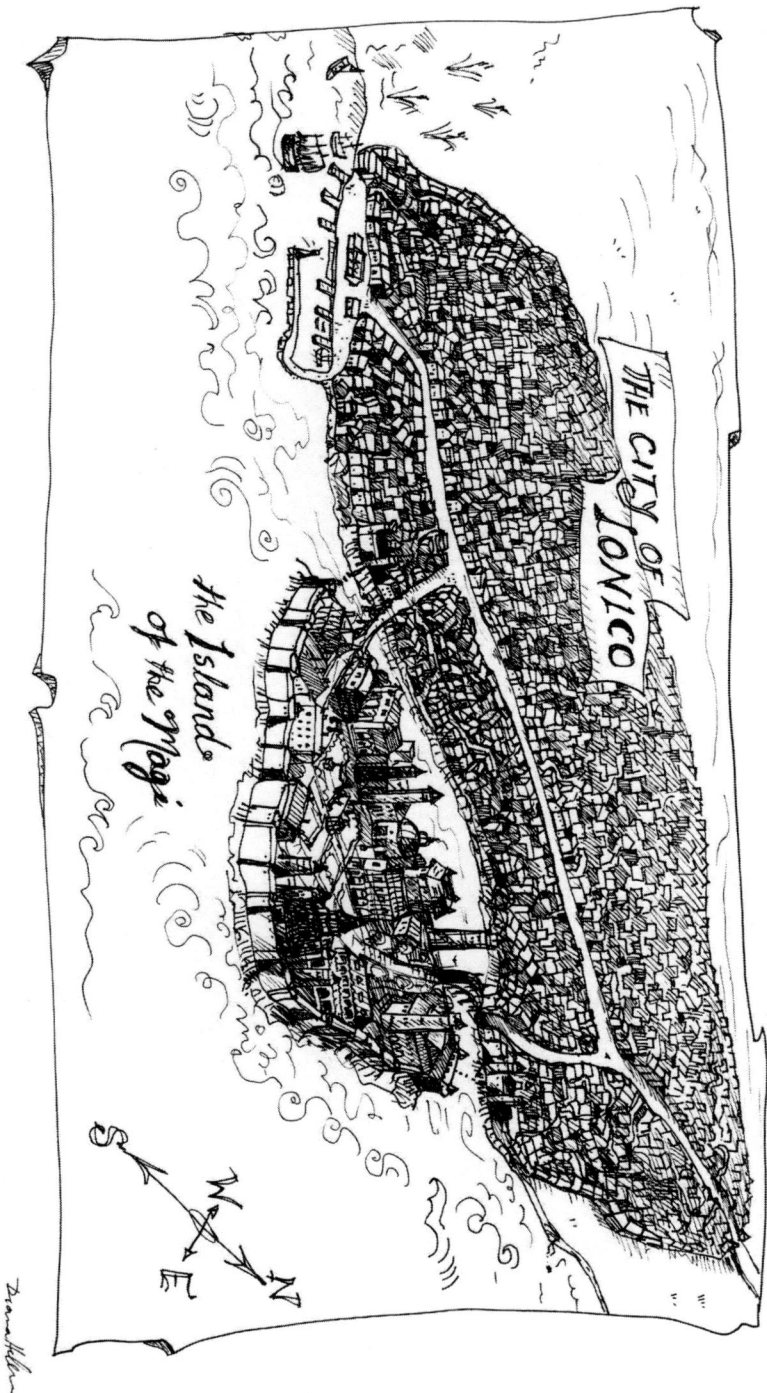

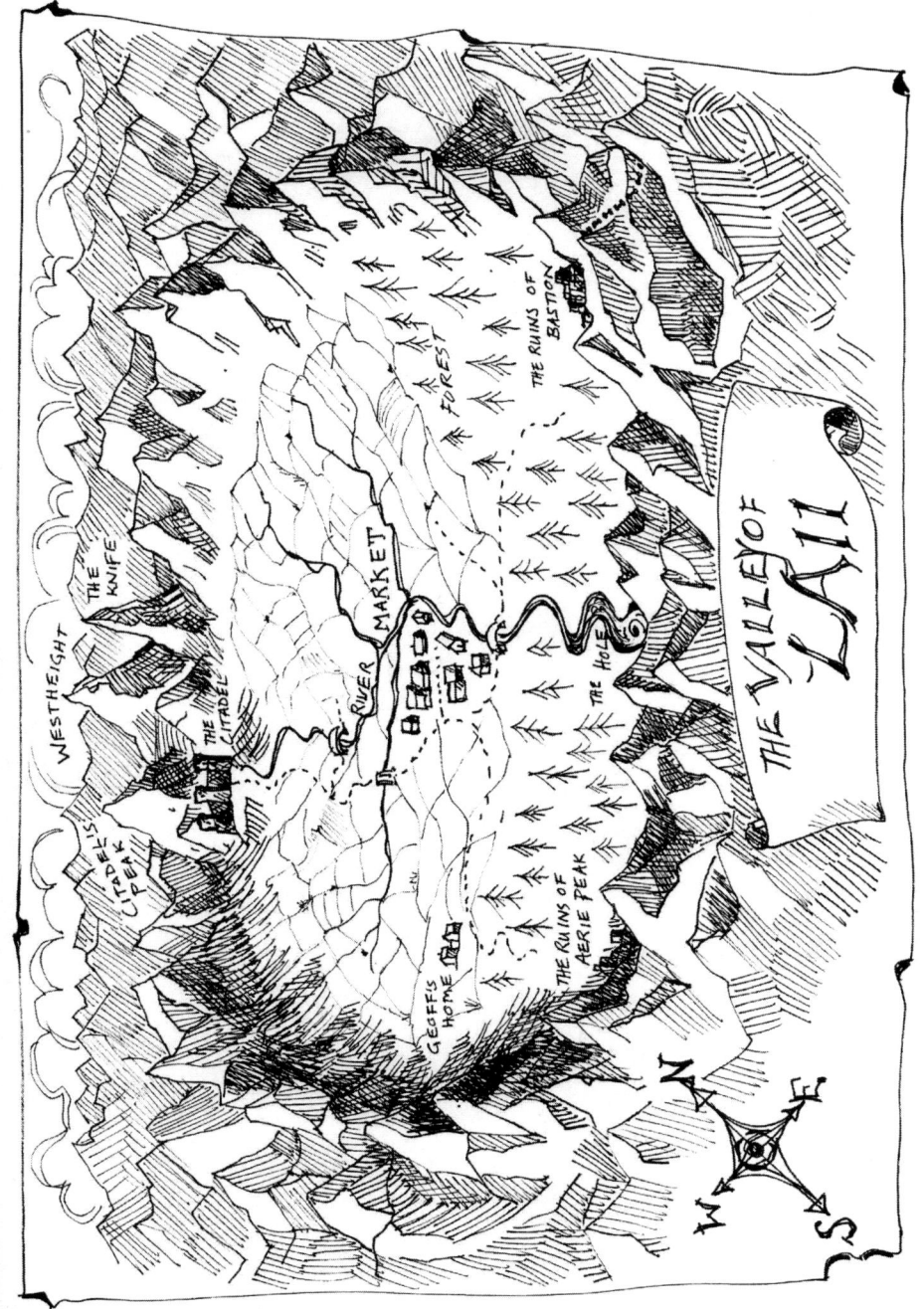

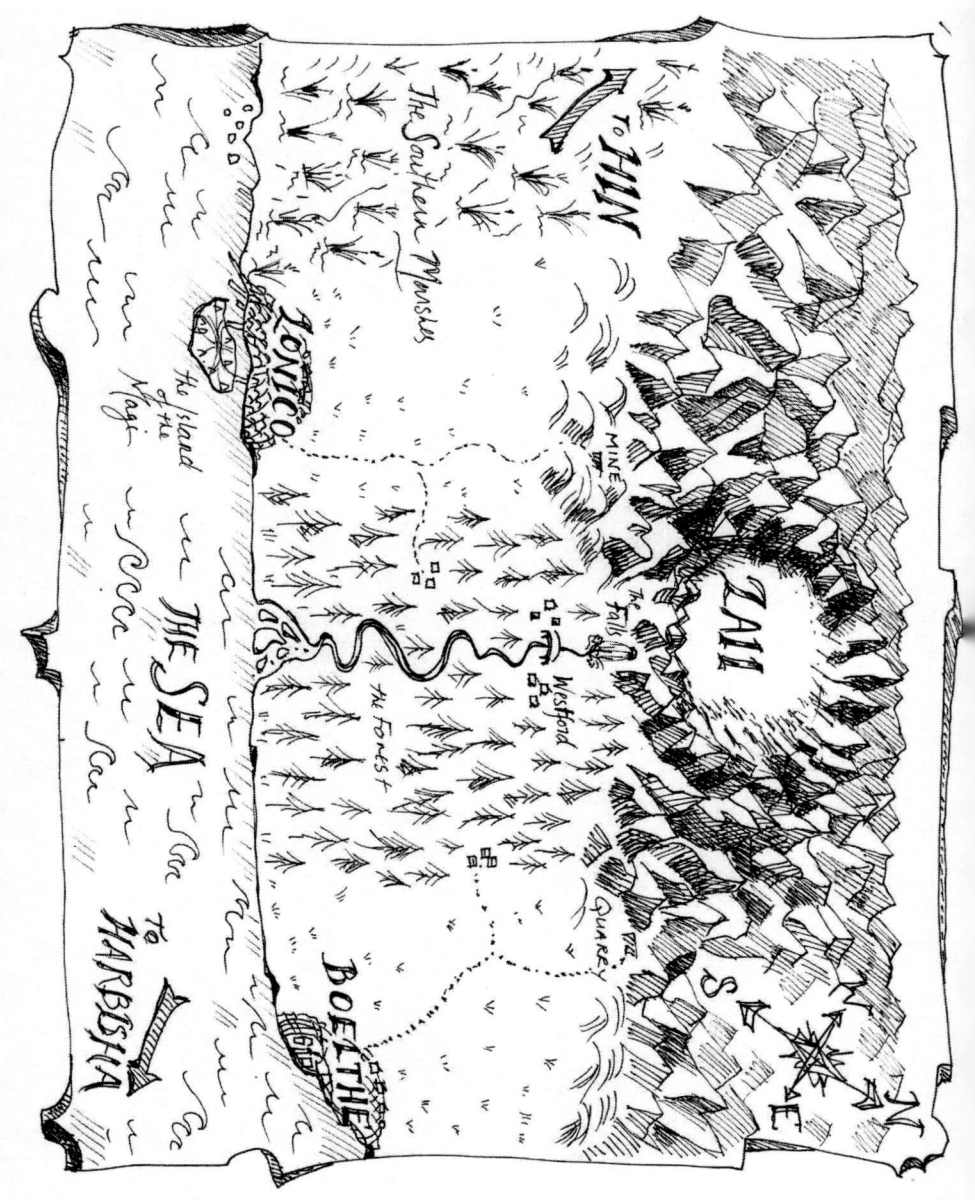

Prologue

"They come at night, you know. Sometimes, when the moon waxes and pulls the sea away from us, one of them gets out and takes a naughty child away. Little children who don't do as they're told get taken by the Laiians and put to work in the mines. If they're lucky children, that is. You don't even want to hear about what happens to the unlucky ones, or to little children who lie to their parents or disrespect the magi. The unlucky ones are dragged from their beds at night and..."

Yachem shrank back from the twisted form of his grandmother and quailed, thrilling at the awfulness of it all. She was a kindly old woman, most of the time, but she obviously relished telling the little boy stories about the monstrous invaders from beyond the mountains – the Laiians. Tales of the inhumans were central to the culture of the city's inhabitants – or at least those parts of the culture that delighted in frightening young children – and on nights like this Yachem's grandmother's eyes glowed with pleasure. Yachem had been hearing this story, and others like it, for as long as he could remember. He never got tired of them, or the rippling shiver they would cause to slide down his spine. The old woman's voice scratched on in the darkness.

"Back in the old days, before the magi, the city was poor. Most Lonicans didn't have shoes to wear – some didn't have food to eat. We were miserable and afraid, and the Laiians were old and powerful even then. They would appear from the west, screaming and gnashing their teeth. They built stacks out of children just like you, then burned them all up – just for fun. They hunted people – people just like you and your mother and your father – for *sport*. When the Laiians came to Lonico the streets were covered in bones, and the sea was red for miles around. Thankfully, eventually the magi appeared and freed us from the monsters forever. The Laiians are trapped in their prison beyond where the sun sets, and they'll stay there as long as the magi are around to protect us."

The woman's voice rasped on. At the rough wooden table across the room, Yachem's mother looked up from her sewing and whispered to her husband.

"Why do you let her tell him those stories? They're terrifying him."

"He's old enough. Would you rather have him ignorant his whole life? Those people were evil. He can't go through life not knowing – there are real monsters out there." Yachem's father shrugged and prodded the fire with an iron poker.

The warm firelight splashed out of the room's single window, marking a span of cobble-stoned street in yellow and red. Winter stood heavy on the throat of the seaside city, and similar pools of light flickered up and down the twisting street – though it barely deserved the name, being hardly more than a crooked crack between houses. Few servants – and fewer magi – cared to brave the wet wind that careened madly down the avenues and alleyways on that night. Here and there a pair of guardsmen hurried along their appointed rounds, barely pausing to glance up from their feet. The call of the warm and bright guard-rooms was too loud, on a night like this, to be ignored for long.

The silent streets of Lonico, narrow and tangled between the few relatively straight avenues, wound their way through the city by the sea. Here and there, vast and ancient bridges reached out over the slate-gray water to a large island studded with towers – also nearly silent in the frigid gloom.

The rolling fields to the west of the city stretched nearly to the feet of the Rim mountains and their hidden, ill-omened vales. All quiet. All still, even in the great forest to the north. As it did every year, the land waited for spring. The world rolled through the seasons, and through the years.

Lonico

1

Geoff rubbed absently at his shoulder as he surveyed the field. A good day's work, he thought – considering all the stones. He could never understand where all the stones came from. Every time the fields were tilled in the spring, there were more damn rocks catching on the ploughshare and wrecking the coulter. Geoff's mood darkened as he unhooked the family donkey from the plough. More damn rocks that had to be torn out of the soil. He tossed the muddy harness carelessly on the ground. Always more damn rocks. He spat at the nearest pile of grey stones, wiped his hands on his rough shirt, and began the long process of dragging the donkey home.

The quarter-mile walk over gently rolling fields took over an hour. Admittedly, Geoff didn't exactly hurry. The donkey didn't help, not with it digging its hooves deep into the soil every forty feet, but neither did the glorious sun setting over the peaks of the western arc of the Rim. Geoff wondered occasionally whether there *was* anything beyond the ring of jagged, broken mountains that surrounded the world. Some of the old stories mentioned places that nobody seemed to be able find in the valley, and occasionally one of the elders claimed that his father's father's father's father's best friend had actually been over the mountains to other places. Nobody Geoff knew had even tried to climb them, however. The Rim was, to all intents and purposes, the end of the world – and nobody but Geoff seemed to care.

As Geoff crested the last little rise before entering his father's farmyard, the donkey suddenly realized it was home and wrenched itself free of his control. It trotted up to the gate and nuzzled at the shoulder of Geoff's brother, Will, who was standing just beyond the low rail fence. Will reached out and patted the donkey's nose affectionately, and then he opened the gate and pointed to the tiny shed that was the animal's home at night. The donkey sauntered over to the shed and went inside. Geoff swore that it winked one gigantic eye at him as it disappeared.

"I hate that thing," Geoff sighed. "It always seems to know exactly what I don't want it to do."

Will laughed. He was twenty, a couple of years older than Geoff, and substantially larger. Neither of the two would ever be considered be considered small or scrawny, but Will was much more thickly roped with muscles. The brothers shared sandy hair and skin that was deeply tanned, wrinkling already from long hours in the fields. They shared little else.

Will was, in Geoff's opinion, slow. He was solid and unspectacular. Undeserving. Infuriatingly unwilling to do the wrong thing, ever. He was also to be the sole inheritor of the farm. On the day Will took control, Geoff would be forced off the land – and essentially sold to another farmer as chattel, reduced to the status of hired help. In a place where every square meter of land was needed, it was a sensible way to do things. Of course, it didn't seem to Geoff that every square meter of land in the Valley *was* needed anymore, but that didn't change the way things were done. It was getting harder and harder to pretend that the day of his eviction wasn't coming – soon. He felt his smile grow stiff on his face, and he turned and walked towards the house.

Inside, the fire cut the chill of the gathering spring evening. Geoff warmed his hands briefly, and nodded to his father. Their relationship, once warm, had grown strained over the last few months as the time of Geoff's departure grew nearer. In the corner Daniel, the farmhand, dozed after a long day's labour. He and Will had been digging a new irrigation trench from the stream that ran just north of the farm. Geoff didn't acknowledge the 'hand. He was still, for another month or so at least, a Son of the farm, while the farmhand was little more than a serf. Geoff's throat tightened at the thought that he would soon be a 'hand on some other plot of land in the valley.

Will paused by the cracking fire to warm his hands and Geoff considered, not for the first time, arranging for an accident to occur. Will could quite easily fall into the river, Geoff reasoned, and this close to the Hole there would be no evidence to show that anything untoward had happened. Geoff suspected that this sort of thing happened sometimes. Certainly there were more than a few second sons

Lonico

in the valley who had suddenly found themselves to be only children. The world was a hard place in more ways than one, and Geoff liked to think that he was far from the softest thing in it. A voice wheezed at him from across the room, and he pulled himself back into the present.

"We need some more wood. Burned through a lot in that snap last month. Tomorrow." The voice fell silent again.

This was his father's way of suggesting that Geoff should add a stack of firewood six feet tall and twelve long to his list of things to do the next day. Geoff sighed inwardly and nodded his acquiescence. He'd never been able to muster any enthusiasm for this sort of mindless, endlessly repeated task. Building a house or barn, sure. That happened rarely, and Geoff could at least *think* about the job he was doing. It was new, a departure from the ordinary slog of life. Unfortunately for Geoff, tasks like chopping wood vastly outnumbered jobs like building houses in the life of a farmer.

Geoff wished that he wasn't a farmer's son. He wished even more strongly that he wasn't a farmer's *second* son. He wished that he could be anything else at all, really. If he'd been born closer to Citadel he could have been apprenticed to old doctor what's-his-name, or to the Priest. If he'd been the Smith's son, he could have lived in Market and spent his days turning the old bits of metal that people occasionally found into useful things like shovels and plough blades.

None of those things were anything more than wishes, however. He had been born clear across the valley from Citadel, in one of the last occupied farms before the edge of the forest that stretched all the way to the eastern Rim. Doctor whoever-he-was had an apprentice and so, he guessed, did the Priest. Geoff *wasn't* the Smith's son. Jacob Smithson would take over from his father eventually, and have a son named Smithson who would take over from him. It was all very tidy, but none of it changed the simple fact that Geoff was about to be tossed out of his home and sent to live like a slave on some other farmer's land. If Geoff ever married – to a younger daughter, perhaps – his eldest son *might* inherit some land, but probably not. At best, though, his other sons would join the farmhand class. If his eldest *did* inherit land, he'd forever be ashamed of his father who was, after all, just a 'hand. It was *such* a *stupid* system. Geoff retained just enough self-awareness to realize that he'd quite like the system – if he was an elder son. He had more than enough anger in him not to care.

Geoff's head began to hurt. He went to bed and lay awake for a long time.

2

The shadows cast by the spires and towers of Lonico heaved crazily on the surface of the sea and reached like a claw across the nearby fields. As the sun rose they retreated into themselves, melting away like icicles in springtime. With the shadows gone a man was revealed sitting on a rock in the middle of the patchwork fields surrounding the city. He was entering early middle-age, his face betraying the strain of some twenty-five years of life in the city, and he was concentrating fiercely on the matter at hand. His dark hair fell repeatedly into his eyes, only to be brushed away by an ink-stained hand. The ink was slowly painting a great black smudge across his forehead and temple – another layer to add to the stratum. No matter how hard he scrubbed, or how hard his wife laughed at him, the ink never quite came clean anymore. He'd have liked to cut his hair, but Taia liked it long, so it stayed as it was. As a result, he had a stripe on his head. Just a price to be paid, he guessed. A quill was clutched awkwardly in a fist obviously still getting used to writing.

"Eight pounds in bag number four."

Yachem silently repeated the words as he wrote them down. Balancing the massive vellum and leather book on his lap, he scratched out the symbols – until recently completely arcane to him. He had been, according to Taia, insufferably pleased to have been chosen to learn this skill. Very few servants were taught to read and write – and those who were taught were almost always destined for positions of high authority. Coming to the end of the phrase, Yachem looked at his master.

The old man was pointing at a leather pouch dangling on the rim of a huge wickerwork basket which was staked to the ground nearby. He gestured impatiently at a heap of stones lying beside the basket, and Yachem saw one of the old man's other servants rush toward the pile. The servant picked up a double-handful of the stones and dropped them one by one into the leather pouch, stopping instantly when the master snarled an order.

"Eight pounds in bag number eight."

Yachem scribbled down the words, trying not to think about the monstrous ... *thing* hanging over his head, and about what he was going to have to do.

The massive basket nearby creaked and settled a little more firmly onto the ground. The sound drew Yachem's attention to it, and to the enormous bag of silk that seemed to be trying to pull the basket up into the sky.

His mind couldn't even conceive of how expensive that bag must have been. Most servants never even *saw* silk up close, let alone owned any. Some of the magi gave their personal servants and concubines tiny squares of silk as marks of favour, and the magi themselves habitually wore silk, of course, but this... this was bigger than a house. There was enough silk here to clothe a small army. The value aside, there was the way the bag was rippling and straining in the gentle morning breeze – like it was alive and unhappy to be tied to the warm earth. The giant contraption wanted to lift into the sky, and Yachem felt physically ill at the wrongness of it. He eyed the thick cables that tethered the basket to the ground and licked his suddenly dry lips.

He was jerked out of his trance by the snap of a finger. His eyes instinctively sought out his master. The old man was glaring at him with red-veined eyes, and jerking his head towards the basket.

"Go," he said, and despite his fears Yachem went.

You didn't argue with the magi. You didn't hesitate. No matter what awaited him in the basket, there was worse to be had from displeasing his master. When the old man said "Go", there was no option but to go. Yachem closed the book and clambered over the rim of the basket. The old man followed him – the servants trying to help him over the basket's high lip without damaging the mage's brittle pride – and sat on the tiny stool in the corner of the basket. He grunted at Yachem, who opened the book and stood ready to take notes.

The mage spoke a few words to the servants gathered before the basket. The men quickly went to work, hatchets in hand. Soon all of the tethers but one, much longer than the others, had been cut. The basket lurched sideways and then staggered into the sky, dragged upwards by whatever demonic force the mage had harnessed.

Yachem shuddered, felt a sudden warmth spread down the inside of his leg, and blanched at the malevolent amusement in his master's eyes as the old man noticed the dark stain.

"Don't ruin my book." The mage's voice was unremarkable, but contained such a promise of sudden and brutal death that Yachem immediately felt more warmth running down his thigh.

"Look over the edge if you wish, Yachem. This is an historic event."

Normally, Yachem would have thrilled and quailed at the prospect of a mage knowing his name, but right now he just lurched obediently to the edge of the basket. He glanced back at his master and saw the old man glaring up at the gigantic silk bag looming over their heads, muttering to himself. Yachem turned and looked as the city spread itself out beneath them. He gaped in wonder and stupefaction.

That is why, although Yachem was the first of the pair to see the squall racing in off the ocean, he said nothing to his master until it was far too late. Yachem's already reeling mind simply couldn't process what he was seeing, and he just stared at the approaching ram of air and water as it surged forward. The storm scattered the tiny boats in the harbor as if they were nothing, roared over the city, and slammed into the basket. Yachem heard —felt— a deep twang as the tether cable snapped in the tumult, and he screamed incoherently as the basket leapt sideways. He saw the mage crumple to the floor of the basket, and lunged to protect the surprisingly frail body with his own. Sobbing with fear, Yachem covered his head with his hands and waited for death.

Lonico

He awoke some time later, shivering uncontrollably. He checked on his master and, finding him still unconscious, peered gingerly over the edge of the basket. Far down and far away, he saw the shape of the seashore and a tiny smudge that might have been the city. In spite of his terror, Yachem could not help but gasp at the beauty of the vista before him. The grasslands before the city shrank into insignificance before the great stretch of the forest to the north, and both were tiny compared to the vast salty marshes to the south – conduit of all of the city's wealth. All of it receded to nothing next to the endless sea beyond.

Yachem marveled at the view for a full fifteen seconds before he realized what must be behind him. He turned slowly, and screamed again. The mage's insane machine was still being swept westward on the winds of the weakening squall, and it was heading towards the mountains.

The treeless peaks loomed closer with every second. The basket was in no immediate danger, as it currently floated higher than the tallest summit, but Yachem wasn't in the least concerned about the mountains themselves. The people who lived *in* the mountains, though, terrified him more than the heights, more than the rocky spires, and more even than the mage lying on the floor of their tiny wicker prison.

A vague memory itched at Yachem's mind. He had not thought of his grandmother in ages. She'd died on Yachem's fifteenth birthday, having lived an incredible fifty-eight years. Her scratchy-soft voice rolled at him like waves now. *The monsters of the valley of the hills. Possessors of magic far more terrible than anything known in the city. Held at bay only by the combined power of the city's magi, exerted in a massive assault hundreds of years ago that had sealed up the valley behind walls of stone.* Walls that Yachem and his master were now drifting over.

Yachem jumped onto his master and shook him, hard – the deeply ingrained reluctance to lay hands on one of the magi of the city overridden by animal terror. The mage's eyes shot open, watery and pink, and he waved Yachem off him with a glare and a snarl. Yachem helped his master to stand and pointed mutely at the peaks.

The old man's rheumy eyes widened and his mouth dropped

agape. He thrust Yachem away and fumbled under his cloak for a second. He shouted something – Yahem couldn't make out the words over the shrieking wind – and raised his hand over his head. There was a repeated crackle-flash and for an instant the eerie stench of magic caught in Yachem's throat. The silk bag shuddered and began to descend, as if forced downwards by a giant hand. Yachem's ears throbbed with the concussive force of the magic and the changing elevation.

The basket's horizontal motion eased fractionally, and the rate of descent increased. The basket sank towards the eastern slopes of the nearest peak. Yachem and the mage relaxed, and glanced at each other. For a moment, collegial feeling filled the dangling basket. For a moment, they were going to make it to the ground before they crested the spine of the mountains.

The moment ended. A sudden gust shoved the bag – basket and men and all – sideways over the rim of peaks. Yachem had time to gape at a primeval forest stretching across a mountain valley before the basket crunched into something, snagged, tilted sideways, tore free from the silk bag, and plummeted towards the earth.

Yachem didn't even feel himself hit the ground.

3

He awoke to find a nut-brown face peering down at him from a darkening sky. It was topped with shaggy, sand coloured hair, and was dominated by a pair of blue eyes – both features completely alien to Yachem. Alien, but drilled into him from his childhood onward as the hallmarks of terror.

"Laiian! Help me, master!"

A moment passed before Yachem recognized the womanly

screech as his own. Tanned skin creased into what could have been the beginning of a frown, and Yachem passed out.

When he awoke, he was immediately aware that he had been moved. The sky was gone entirely, replaced by log beams and rough-hewn planks. The horrible face of his tormentor was not immediately visible, for which he was immensely grateful. He tried to turn his head and almost screamed. As various parts of his body began to throb and ache, Yachem realized that every bit of him hurt. He was also aware that his right arm and leg were lying in strange and awkward positions. They seemed to have too many bends in them, somehow.

That realization brought on the pain, which brought on the screams in earnest.

Like a carrion bird to a beached fish, his tormentor appeared. This time two other Laiians joined him, one substantially older and more terrifying than either of the others. The one who had found him in the forest was muttering to the eldest, who nodded along as he listened. The old one gestured at something right in the corner of Yachem's field of view, and Yachem saw the shredded remains of the basket slumped in a far corner of the room.

"No choice I guess. Take him. Tomorrow."

Yachem quailed at the idea of being taken anywhere. He knew that he was in no shape to resist, however, so he merely whimpered. He was in so much pain that it didn't even occur to him to ask about his master. Eventually exhaustion numbed the agony a bit, and a fractured sleep took him.

The next few days were nightmarish. Drifting in and out of a stupor, Yachem swung between dreams of looping flights through silken clouds and those of being beaten with leather bags full of rocks. Occasionally he'd imagine that he was tumbling downhill towards a precipice. He'd scream and scrabble at the sliding ground, but to no avail. Nightmarish wraiths with blue eyes and ill-kempt blond hair hounded him. They danced through his dreams like gulls – no, they *were* gulls – no, they were the master, displeased because Yachem was writing too slowly – now his grandmother cackling and gibbering and rending her clothing and screaming at him to run – now Taia, his new wife waiting for him back in the City, laughing at his pathetic mewling. Now they were Laiians, and he'd fallen from the sky into the valley of the monsters of the mountains.

Suddenly the dreams ceased, and Yachem found himself securely strapped to a cart. He was lying on his back, his legs and arms bound with leather bands. He could smell the animal (a donkey, it turned out) that was pulling the cart along a bumpy track or road. He groaned, and saw one of his tormentors look over a burlap-clad shoulder at him. A voice, half-heard against the thump-rumble-groan of the cart, reached his ears.

"… fever's broke."

An answering grunt could have meant "good" or "we'll see about that" or any number of other things.

Yachem, still dazed, still sick, still broken, marveled for a moment at the Laiians' coarse language. He'd known that they must be savages — nothing else could explain the stories he'd heard — but for a society of diabolical warrior-magi these people sounded a lot like the farmers whose holdings ringed the city, providing it with what food the sea could not.

Hope rose up for a moment in Yachem's chest. Had it all been a dream? Could he have landed on the mountains' eastern slopes after all? He almost giggled. The flash of a blue eye from one of the figures in the front of the cart, however, turned the laugh cold in his throat. No Lonican had eyes that colour. The Laiian — the one who had first found Yachem, he now realized — turned in his seat and regarded the servant coldly. There was something in that gaze that reminded Yachem of the magi, for a moment. Something calculating and cold glinted in that eye. Yachem was glad when the Laiian looked away.

Lonico

4

Daniel felt Geoff turn away from their passenger and back to the road. The young man — still a boy, really — had seemed different ever since he'd come back to the farmhouse that night, with the donkey behind him towing a wrecked basket and a flabby man with pale skin and eerily dark eyes.

Before that night, Daniel would have said that Geoff was a bit unhappy about being forced to leave the farm that autumn. It was a hard thing, Daniel knew, to be told to leave your home — to be told that you were now, more or less, somebody else's problem. It hadn't been easy for Daniel himself to accept it, when it had happened to him, and he considered himself to be a fairly even-tempered man. He thought about that for a while, and decided that he was correct. He *was* a fairly even-tempered man.

The transition from Son of the farm to 'hand was a hard one. Daniel had gotten lucky, of course. Geoff's father Benjamin was the kindliest of masters and the most doting of parents — Daniel had no doubt that he was working hard to find Geoff a good home. Daniel had tried to talk about things with Geoff, to cheer him up, but the young man hadn't seemed to be ready for that yet. Ah well. All in its time.

Ever since the night Geoff had dragged that basket and its passenger through the door of the farmhouse, however, he'd been a changed man. Gone was the quiet boy of the past. There seemed to be a new life to him, now. Like he'd figured something out. Daniel nodded inwardly. The boy probably just wanted some excitement before he settled into his new life. That was understandable. Daniel himself had tried to swim the Hole — twice — just before he'd been sent from his old home to Benjamin's.

Graham Angus

This trip to Citadel would be just the thing for the young man. He'd get to be at the center of things for a while as they nursed the broken stranger back to health, and then he'd be happy to get on with his life.

Idly, Daniel wondered where the odd-looking man in the wagon had come from. There weren't any farms off in the direction Geoff had found them in – the area was part of the valley's carefully managed forest – and the stranger was paler than a Market-man. Maybe he was a hermit from down near the Aerie Peak ruins or something. At any rate, the doctor at Citadel would set him right. Hopefully. Even folks who weren't quite, you know, *right* deserved better than to be broken into bits like the fellow in the back of the wagon.

Daniel tried, again, to figure out why the man had been found with such a big basket – and how he'd ended up on the ground under it. Had he been living *up* a tree? Pleased with his theory, Daniel started to sing an old song to himself as he encouraged the donkey to pull them just a little faster.

He didn't know what sugar was, or a ship, but he liked the sound of the ancient nonsense words anyway.

The road rolled away under their cart as they bounced and jolted along towards Citadel. Their going was slow. The donkey-drawn cart was never the fastest thing in the valley, and Daniel was driving slowly to minimize their passenger's discomfort. The road curved and jogged along the hilly floor of the valley, climbing slowly towards the Citadel built right up against the western Rim. Daniel didn't know why anyone had ever wanted to build such a thing. Apparently he wasn't alone – the vast building had long since fallen to ruins, and much of the hard mountain stone that had been used in its construction had been carted away and put to better use.

Only the priests and the doctor lived there now, in a small collection of houses built against – and of – one massive wall of the structure. There were farms nearby, of course, and everyone in the valley sent a small amount of supplies to the west every year. You never knew when you'd need a doctor. Or a priest. It was, quite simply, the way it was *done* – and it would never have occurred to Daniel to have questioned the way it was done, even if he'd driven back and forth along the rutted valley road every day of his life.

Lonico

"How much longer?"

Geoff's high, liquid voice pierced Daniel's reverie, and brought that part of him which wasn't monitoring the fatigue of the donkey, charting a path between the deeper potholes on the road, or trying to identify an annoying and repeated squeal in one of the wheels back from the daydream. He took his eyes off of the road for a moment and flicked them toward the farmer's son. Geoff's cool blue eyes were regarding him evenly.

"Ah..." Daniel quickly took his bearings. They were passing through a small but dense thicket of trees – known as Holtom's wood despite the fact that it was barely eighty feet wide and none of the trees were more than twenty feet tall. They had left the falling-down barn behind them about half an hour ago. After this would be the stream, and then the last hill to Citadel. "... not long now. You ought to see the tower as soon as we're out of the wood. Might be a bit hard to pick out against the Rim, but it'll be there. I'd say we'll be about another hour or so. Just in time to stable the donkey and see to the wagon before supper."

Daniel's companion grunted and turned his gaze to their passenger again. The 'hand shrugged and brought his attention back to the road as it curled to the north. The trees suddenly thinned out as the cart reached the edge of the wood, and before them lay one of the valley's great vistas.

A silvery creek ran and looped between patchy fields towards the River to the north of them, crossed by a low stone bridge wide enough to drive six carts across at once. The bridge was made of the black mountain stone of the Rim Mountains, and despite being older than anyone could remember, showed no ruts from the dozens of carts that must have crossed it every month for all of time. Beyond the bridge, the dusty road of the valley floor wound back and forth up the gentle face of a grassy hill. Here and there, chunks of mountain stone too large to have been easily carted away still showed through the dirt scrawl of the road. Daniel's grandfather had maintained that the whole valley road had once been made of flagstones, but that time, weather, and scavenging by the valley's residents had reduced the road to little more than a dirt track.

Graham Angus

Daniel remembered sitting at his grandfather's knee and asking why anyone had bothered to build a road out of stone. The old man had shifted in his chair and said that obviously they had a lot of extra stone back then. Daniel's grandfather had hated not knowing the answer to any question put to him, so he always made sure to know everything. It was said in the family that he'd never once been wrong about anything, a fact about which Daniel was justifiably proud. Not many people could claim that their grandfather had been infallible.

Farther up the hill in the blue distance, right at the level where the green grass gave over to black stone, reared the tall tower and massive walls of the Citadel. The walls were easily twenty-five feet tall and still imposing after neglect that extended back beyond living memory. The tower stood an additional thirty feet above the walls and loomed over the entire eastern valley. They said that from the top of it you could see all the way to Market, but Daniel didn't believe them. A spring welled up inside the walls of Citadel, and water poured endlessly out of a cunningly carved stone face on the eastern, undisturbed wall of the building. The water sluiced down the hill near the road, and eventually joined up with the silvery cord of the creek at the bottom of the slope. Daniel stopped the wagon where the two streams came together, to allow the donkey to drink in the cold water and Geoff to drink in the view. A boy's first trip to Citadel was always something special. Although it was tucked away against the Rimwall, almost abandoned and completely ineffable, the great stone building was in many ways the center of the valley.

Daniel walked around to the rear of the cart and checked on the strange pale man whose sudden arrival had sent them on this journey. He was staring up at the dark building that dominated the area.

"Whasthat?"

It took Daniel a few seconds to decipher the strange phrase. When he did, he realized that the man had asked him what 'that' was – and he'd spoken very quickly. Daniel turned his head and followed the man's shaking finger. Did he really not recognize the building?

"That's Citadel. The Citadel. Do you not know it?"

Daniel had no idea why the stranger passed out again. He turned to Geoff.

"I think we'd best hurry. He seems to have taken another turn."

Lonico

5

Yachem regained what was left of his senses just as the cart crested the top of the hill. He blinked tears out of his eyes and peered around him. The hill they had just climbed must have been several hundred feet tall, and the ground veered precipitously away from the back of the cart towards the valley floor. The hill was higher than the tallest tower of the City by at least a ship's length, and the jolting shudder of the wagon was too much like the basket's final terrifying moments for Yachem's comfort. He began to feel his stomach giving way again.

He was so tired of that. Yachem could remember, vaguely, a time when he'd been more than a quivering wreck of a man. A time before the master had gestured at a wicker basket and told him to get into it. Yachem had been a valued and well cared-for servant of the magi, once. He had been taught to read! He had been singled out, he knew, for great things. He had been chosen for a position of responsibility, and of health, and of safety – of privilege and relative comfort. Of course, now that was all a distant memory. Yachem's only source of solace was the sure knowledge that he'd soon have his liver cut out and eaten in front of him, or be forced to pull out his own intestines with a hook, or he'd simply be set on fire and murdered, or any one of a hundred similar things that his grandmother had warned him would happen if he was ever caught by Laiians, and then it would all be over. He would die and it would be over. Hopefully his good service would allow him to be reborn as an even more highly-placed servant.

If, he suddenly thought, his spirit could even find its way back to the city from here. If it wasn't torn from him and shredded in the teeth of some mountain demon. Yachem whimpered. He barely noticed the cart turn away from the Citadel's massive gates and trundle towards a small group of buildings huddled low against the eastern wall of the crumbling fortress.

The cart groaned to a halt, and for a moment the only sound was the laboured breathing of the exhausted donkey. The wind pawed at Yachem's hair. The cart shifted as the two Laiians clambered to the ground. While the larger of the two walked towards the donkey and began to remove the harness that bound it to the cart, the smaller man – the one with the cold eyes – moved into a nearby doorway, and Yachem seized his chance. Summoning the shreds of strength that he'd regained over the days of his enforced inactivity, Yachem slipped free of the leather straps securing him to the cart, heaved himself over the edge, staggered to the crest of the hill, and threw himself down the incline. If he could get far enough away from them, maybe they'd be unwilling or unable to pursue him. Failing that, he could only hope to die in the attempt, his body and spirit undefiled by the twisted magic of the mountain people.

Yachem bounded down the slope, leaping from rock to tuffet, his feet slipping and scrabbling as moist earth and lush grasses tore away from the hillside. There was a measure of joy in this, he thought. It would be a good way to die, and would keep his spirit singing as it wended the grey paths home. He heard the sound of distant shouts behind him, and tried to move more quickly. In his haste, Yachem's right foot landed on a patch of loose stones and shot out from under him. He pitched forwards, his balance utterly gone, and began to tumble down the hill. It was about to happen. He was about to be free. He almost laughed in anticipation. Those monsters would have to look somewhere else for a victim.

Fate refused to co-operate with Yachem on this occasion, as it had on so many others in the recent past. The yielding ground cushioned every impact, and the gently shallowing curve of the hill's base slowed his descent comfortably. He came rolling to a halt just short of the burbling stream running blithely downwards into the valley proper. Mustering what little equilibrium and strength he still possessed, Yachem half-crawled, half-slithered towards the water. He plunged his head and shoulders into the stream, opened his mouth to take a breath – and was tugged backwards out of the frigid water.

Lonico

Looking up, he saw the form of the larger of the two Laiians leaning over him. He could feel the stone weight of the man's hands pressing down into his chest, pinning him to the ground. Over the terrifying man's shoulders, Yachem made out the form of two others bounding down the hill towards him, whooping and calling.

"Why'd you do that damn fool thing? Trying to get yourself killed?" The man shook Yachem by the shoulders.

The two other Laiians drew to halt and stared down at Yachem and his torturer. The young one with the burning eyes murmured something to the new one. The new one was older. His face was paler than the other two, and covered with a web of tiny wrinkles. He was a massive man, but one shrinking into old age. Gigantic shoulders were beginning to waste away, but there was still a sense of power about his carriage, and a deep understanding in his eyes. He looked like a mage to Yachem, albeit one that was dressed all in dark wools rather than silks.

He stared down at Yachem with something indecipherable in his eyes. Pity? That didn't make any sense at all, unless the fate in store for the servant was something that even the soulless Laiians balked at. Yachem lost himself in the horror of that line of thought for a few minutes, and when his mind returned to the present he was back at the top of the hill, being carried through a low wooden door and down a cold-rock hallway. He was placed, not ungently, on a pallet inside the cool building and the closing of the door to the brightness outside struck Yachem temporarily blind.

The thudding of boots striking a stone floor. The creak of wood straining under a substantial weight. The sudden glare of an uncovered lamp. Yachem looked around. The room in which he now lay was tiny. There were no windows, and only the one door. A cell. The furnishings were simple. The pallet – which smelled, startlingly, clean – a small stool, and a large table with a clay lamp on it completed the appointments.

Sitting on the stool and looking keenly at Yachem was the massive mage in the woolen robe. The man was leaning forward with his hands on his knees and peering at Yachem's twisted leg. Yachem sighed internally. He'd probably forfeited any chance of ever walking again with his escape attempt. Even if he was ever allowed to stand again, he could *feel* that something was very much worse inside than it had been before. The pain was just starting to grow, but Yachem was sure that it would soon overwhelm him.

The man prodded experimentally at Yachem's arm and leg, provoking agonized gasps. He shook his head slightly, stood, and left the room – footsteps echoing ever-quieter into silence. Yachem relaxed into his pallet for a moment, glad of the solitude, and the quiet, and the small lamp forcing the darkness into inky cowering shadows in the corners of the room. Yachem lay there for what could have been a moment, or a minute, or an hour before he once again heard the scuff of boots in the hallway.

The door opened, and the three Laiians strode into the room. Yachem would have huddled in the corner with the shadows if he'd been able, but was forced to content himself with a tiny whimper. The Laiian mage carried with him a bowl of steaming sour liquid that was unceremoniously poured down Yachem's throat, his protests silenced and struggles stilled by the iron grip of Laiian hands. Yachem spluttered for a moment before he noticed that someone had opened a hole in the bottom of his foot and drained all of the pain from his body. He tried to gather the energy to find the hole and plug it so that his soul didn't run out too, but it was so much easier just to lie back. The Laiians were tugging at Yachem's injured arm and leg and it hurt, but no sooner was the pain recognized by the long-suffering servant than it slipped away and was gone.

Yachem heard some rather loud cracking sounds, and then a voice spoke quietly. "Fogstem. Very effective against pain. Even the shock of having that shoulder re-located and his leg set won't really have made an impact on him right now."

Yachem wondered who they were talking about as he drifted off into a blissful slumber.

He didn't know how long he'd slept. The pain in his arm and leg – and of his other injuries – seemed to have been lessened, and what pain there was seemed to be somehow *healthier*. The pain of knitting bones and mending muscles rather than newly broken, shredded ones. Yachem moved his stiff limbs and found that they were securely splinted. Strong and very slightly springy wood was lashed to his right arm and leg with some sort of cord – not the hempen rope common in the City, but something that seemed almost translucent and a little elastic. Catgut or something like it, he thought. Other than his splints, Yachem noticed that he wasn't restrained in any way. There was a plate piled high with dark bread on the small table, and an earthen jug of something sweet-smelling beside it. Furthermore, the door was slightly ajar. Faint noises echoed through the opening, loud enough to tell Yachem only that he was not alone in the building.

Levering himself upright, Yachem staggered to the table and fell upon the food. Cramming handfuls of bread into his mouth and washing them down with the sweet, slightly warm drink in the mug, Yachem cleaned the plate quickly. Only when he was sure that he'd eaten every crumb and drunk every drop did Yachem turn his attention towards the door. Hobbling towards it he peered, cautiously, around the doorframe. A hallway, built out of massive slabs of black stone, faded away into darkness to his right, punctured by a couple of massive doorways. To Yachem's left, the hallway came to an abrupt end as it opened into a room both larger and brighter than his own cell. Multi-hued glassed windows pierced the walls. Yachem's jaw dropped. In the City, only the richest buildings of any sort possessed coloured glass. The method for making it was so expensive and time-consuming that it was reserved exclusively for the homes and edifices of the magi. A huge fire was burning in a stone fireplace, and a large pot of something hung near it, bubbling gently and spreading a savory smell through the room. Yachem was startled to find that his hunger had returned, stronger than ever. He inched into the chamber, all other concerns forced aside by the thought of whatever was in that ironware pot. His single-mindedness ended, however, as he stepped into the center of the room. He was suddenly aware of the absence of a sound that had not even registered in his conscious mind until now: a quiet conversation had just come to a halt.

Yachem's head swung to the right, to an area of the room previously out of sight behind the corner. Sitting around an ancient and massive wooden table were the three Laiians, and all of them were looking at him. The wrinkled one who looked like a mage muttered something to the youngest of the men – the one who'd found him in the woods, the one with the cold blue eyes – who rose from his bench and walked towards the fire. Yachem watched, drool pooling in his mouth, as the young Laiian ladled a wooden bowl full of thick soup and carried it back to the table. The eldest, the mage, gestured to Yachem.

"Come. Sit with us. You must be famished."

Yachem bobbed his head, his hunger and natural deference to authority vastly out-muscling the lingering shreds of fear which clung to his heart. He hobbled to the table and heaved himself down onto a bench beside the wrinkle-faced mage.

"My master? What happened to him?" The three Laiians looked at each other briefly, and the mage spoke, quietly.

"Time enough for that. Enjoy your food first." The man indicated the youngest Laiian, and then the third one, the one who'd pulled Yachem from the stream.

"This is Geoff, and this Daniel. I am called Doctor, although it's more of a title than a name. You may call me Samuel, if you prefer. Eat your food. We'll be taking you to see Priest soon, and there will be time enough for questions and answers then."

6

Geoff drummed his fingers on the heavy oak tabletop as he watched the stranger eat the simple vegetable stew that the doctor had prepared. The man was having trouble with the splints that had been put on him. His movements with his unencumbered left arm were jerky and unpracticed – he was obviously right handed – and his walking was similarly inexpert with his right leg bound into unbending straightness. He wasn't in any kind of shape to try anything, and he was in the safest hands in the valley with Doctor Samuel looking after him, which begged the question that Geoff now voiced.

"Why are we still here, Doctor? Can't you take care of him on your own?"

Geoff had more than enough problems on his hands, he thought, what with the fact that he was about to be thrown out of his home and turned into a servant. He wanted to get back to the farm and figure out some sort of plan – if there was anything to be done at all.

Daniel's mouth dropped open at the sheer effrontery of Geoff's question, but the Doctor just smiled.

"Don't you," he asked, "want to hear his story? I suspect that it may well be the most interesting thing you've ever heard."

Geoff thought about that for a moment. It's true that the stranger was interesting, after a fashion. It was also true that he didn't for a moment believe Daniel's idea that the man (and his dead companion) had been living up a tree in the eastern forest. More importantly, Geoff reasoned, every day that passed before he went home was another day of delay before the eventual reckoning that stripped him of his status as a Son of a farm.

"Alright," he sighed. "We'll stay and hear him out. What do you think he's going to say?"

The Doctor simply shrugged and returned to his study of the pasty stranger, who was still spooning great gobs of soupy stew into his mouth like he was afraid that it might be his last meal in this world. Whatever suspicions Samuel had, thought Geoff, he was apparently going to keep to himself for now.

Several large bowls of soup later the stranger's pace of consumption began to slow, and eventually he stopped eating altogether. He laid the spoon he'd been using on the table with exaggerated care and leaned back against the wall, his good arm draped across the bulge of his full stomach. He was, by Valley standards, a rather fat man – which is to say that he was not entirely composed of tough-knotted muscle, stretched sinew, and gnarled bones. His unhealthy pallour, perhaps heightened by the constant pain that he must be in, highlighted the strange darkness of his hair and eyes, and the odd black smear across his forehead. Geoff noted, however, that those eyes were not entirely bereft of intelligence, and Doctor said that the smear was likely made of something called 'ink' – an unfamiliar word, but one that the old man seemed to think was significant. The stranger might be smarter than he'd so far appeared – not a difficult feat, as he'd spent most of the time since Geoff had found him screaming and fainting and attempting to run away from people who were just trying to help him.

The fire crackled against the cool spring evening. The stranger had slept through a night and the entire day after it before he'd emerged, but already looked less frantic, less injured, less *damaged*. The quiet was marked only by the popping of sparks; the near-constant scraping of spoon against bowl and slurping of soup had faded into memory. The four men sat for a long time without speaking. Somewhere, from deep in the bowels of the building, a bell chimed. The Doctor stood.

"It's time to go see Priest, gentlemen."

Samuel and Daniel helped the stranger to his feet, and Daniel supported the pale man as the foursome walked slowly down dark and twisting hallways, lower and lower until Geoff was certain that they must be far underground. Certainly the only illumination came from the guttering lamp that the Doctor carried with him, carving a tiny mobile cave of brightness out of the darkness.

"Where are we going?"

Geoff's question echoed once off the walls and then seemed to go flat and deaden, muffled by the earth and the living stone of Citadel. Even the noise of their footsteps was swallowed up almost immediately by the stone walls – as if the fortress had heard too many sounds over the course of its existence, and lacked the energy to acknowledge these new ones.

"The vaults," replied the Doctor. "Priest said that he needed to do some reading before he met us. He's been down here since you arrived. We're under the old Citadel, now. Few of these rooms are used at all anymore – there are just four of us living here, after all, and we only need so much space."

The interminable march came to an abrupt end when Samuel,

passing a door that looked no different from any of the others they'd walked by, swung to his right and pounded twice on the thick wood.

A voice called faintly from beyond the door.

"Come in, Doctor."

The Doctor reached for the handle and paused. Turning, he addressed Geoff and Daniel.

"You may learn things in here that surprise you. Priest can answer your questions, but it would be best if you didn't go spreading what you learn here around. You'll understand why, hopefully, and if you don't – ask." The wide-shouldered man gripped the door handle, twisted, and shoved the door open.

Geoff gaped at the sight beyond the doorway, and he heard Daniel gasp aloud. The stranger seemed to shrink a little back into himself, as if a bit of the old fear was returning. Geoff followed the Doctor into the room, leaving Daniel to drag the suddenly recalcitrant stranger in behind them. His eyes hardly knew where to rest. The room must have been sixty feet tall. It was roughly square, and ringed by tiers of deep balconies. Massive columns rose from the floor, some looped around by iron stairways, leading up to the upper stories. The room was lit like mid-day. A group of windows at the top of the room fed light into an array of angled mirrors that reflected the waning evening light across and around the entire room. There was barely a shadow to be seen, and the contrast between the night-dark hallway and this room could not have been more striking. All three of the levels were lined from floor to ceiling with shelves packed with bulging strips of leather – and Geoff could see that the nearest ones had golden markings on them. They looked tremendously valuable, extraordinarily old, and utterly unfamiliar.

"Doctor, what *are* those things? What *is* this place?"

Incredibly, it was the pale and injured stranger who answered, in a shaking, fear-filled voice.

"Those are called books. This place is a library."

Geoff and Daniel looked at the stranger blankly, and the Doctor shot him an amused look. A voice snapped the reverie.

"You're quite right, of course. It's mostly ruined now, but in its time this was one of the world's great libraries."

Graham Angus

Geoff and Daniel swung their heads towards the new speaker. He was a slim, almost willowy man, perhaps six or seven years older than Geoff himself. He was dressed much like the Doctor was – a simple black robe and soft shoes. His eyes were a paler blue even than Daniel's, and his closely cropped hair was golden. He projected an air of calm, and Geoff saw the stranger relax a trifle in Daniel's grip.

He smiled – a bit sadly, Geoff thought – and introduced himself.

"My name is Priest. I understand that you're called Geoff Benjaminson, and you are Daniel," a pair of quick nods confirmed this, "but I'm not sure if I've heard your name yet." Priest's blue eyes turned to look at the pale man.

The stranger looked Priest in the eyes and sagged slightly.

"My name is Yachem."

"Well, Yachem," Priest gestured the group towards a group of chairs around a table in the center of the room, "perhaps you'd care to tell us how you came to be found lying next to a dead man in a basket under a tree in the far eastern end of the valley."

Geoff saw Yachem's face pale as he absorbed the news of his master's death. He was full of questions on the matter, after he recovered, and was only slightly calmed by Geoff and Daniel's assurances that the old man had been given a good burial. Eventually the questions stopped, and Priest asked Yachem once again to tell the story of his arrival in the valley.

Geoff listened with growing scorn as Yachem told his tale. It was all so ridiculous. A City (whatever *that* meant – Market's thirty houses were far and away the largest settlement that Geoff had ever heard of) beside an Ocean (hah!) ruled by magi (ha hah!) – *beyond the Eastern Rim!* Yachem would have had better luck claiming to be a very tall apple, and Geoff told him so in no uncertain terms. He was just getting warmed up to his subject when he noticed that Priest and Doctor were looking at him far too quietly, and also that Daniel was repeatedly stomping on Geoff's foot under the table. Geoff's tirade drifted to an uncertain halt.

"It all just sounds so … silly," he finished lamely. "I mean, there's nothing else out there, is there? The valley *is* the world. The Rim is

Lonico

the End. Isn't ... it?"

Priest shook his head. "The records are a bit sketchy. A lot of our knowledge was lost long ago, and more is lost every year to bookworms or rot, but I do know that there is more to the world than the valley. We used to be connected to it, too. Citadel was built to guard the western pass into to the valley, and there were other fortresses at Aerie Peak and Bastion that guarded the eastern ones. Hundreds of years ago, there was a war, and our enemies sealed the three entrances to the valley, trapping most of our people inside. What happened to our King and his family we don't know. Trapped outside and killed by our homeland's enemies, most likely. Since then, things have... gotten harder with every generation, apparently. Now, most of us don't even remember that it was ever any different."

"Why would they do that? Seal us in here, I mean." Daniel's question was plaintive, and Priest merely shrugged. Yachem, however, nearly snarled.

"Our magi sealed you in here because you were monsters! You killed and raped and burned your way across the world until the magi were able to contain you in here, and they maintain eternal vigilance against the day when you break out!"

Priest raised his hands in a placating gesture. "That may be – or it may be that your history has changed as much as ours has in the intervening centuries. I don't know. Our oldest books, the ones from before the valley's sealing, speak of our people as traders, not conquerors. Again, however, I don't know. Either story could be true. Or neither. Or part of both. If what you've told us is true, however, it's obvious that we don't pose much of a threat to your city any more, Yachem. We are only farmers now, and barely hanging on as it is."

Priest gestured at a column of markings inked onto a sheet of heavy paper before him. "These," he said, "represent all of the people in the valley. Do you know numbers as well as words, Yachem?"

The stranger nodded, and Priest pushed the paper across the table. Yachem stared at it intently for a few minutes, and looked up, shock writ plain on his face.

"Are these numbers accurate?"

Priest spread his hands. "Every one. When you attend every marriage, every funeral, and every birthing as we do," he indicated the Doctor and himself, "there's little chance of error. At my last count, there are just over fifteen hundred people living in the Valley. Thirty years ago, there were seventeen hundred. Two hundred years ago, there were probably five thousand people living in Citadel alone. This valley is dying – or at least the humans in it are. By the time your children die, Geoff, there may be nobody left to replace them. That's why we need to go for aid *now*, while there are still enough of us that we don't get swamped by a flood of immigrants and forgotten, or simply die away like a breeze in evening-time. That's why I need your help, Yachem. We cannot continue as things are. I – we – need you to return home and convince your magi to re-open the passes to the valley. We need trade, and new blood, and we need them soon or we'll wither away into nothing."

Yachem was silent for a while, and when he spoke his voice was quiet. "I don't think that you understand. I am no mage. I am a servant, and in the halls of the magi my voice is quieter than the sound of the wind. They would not even listen to me even if I asked them to help you. With my master dead in my care, I may even be summarily hung upon my return to the city."

Priest was silent for a time. "I thought that might be the case. If so, and if you choose, you are welcome to accompany me as I make the journey."

Daniel cocked his head to one side. "You had already decided to go," he said.

Priest nodded. "At the last council, it was agreed that I should go this summer or next anyway, but with actual proof that people outside the valley still exist and a guide quite literally falling into my lap, the timing could not be better."

Everything unrolled in front of Geoff's eyes. Suddenly there was a way to escape his fate. To make something of himself not based on simple-minded drudgery. To be someone. To show up that insufferable bastard Will.

"I'd like to come too, Priest. There's nothing for me here."

Geoff couldn't read the quick look that flashed between Priest and Doctor Samuel, but was relieved when Priest shrugged and nodded. Beside him, he heard Daniel shift and clear his throat.

"Don't bother," hissed Geoff. "Your presence will not be necessary."

Daniel raised his eyebrows. "My responsibility is to you. Your father told me so, and he'd hardly think it proper that I let you wander off beyond the Rim without someone to watch your back. Never know what these people from out-valley are going to be like. No offense meant, Mr. Yachem, but I wouldn't be surprised if they were stranger than Market men."

Geoff barely managed a smile at Daniel's attempted joke – if that's what it was. Daniel might actually think that he was just being polite. The suggestion that Geoff still needed a babysitter smarted, though. He was almost a man now, and the last thing he needed was some 'hand following him all over the valley and beyond. There was nothing for it, though, short of ordering the man to stay behind in front of Priest and Yachem and the Doctor. Geoff's credibility in their eyes would be destroyed if Daniel refused the order, which he just might. *Damn.*

As Samuel, Priest, Yachem and even Daniel planned the expedition, Geoff sat in silence. The mirror-caught light shed the pale pink of a spring evening-time, and eventually gave up its daily war against the darkness.

7

Daniel stretched and scuffed sleep from his eyes as he watched the sun rise over the distant peaks of the eastern Rim. This far to the west, tucked up against the western Rim itself, the sunrise came earlier and more gradually than it did at Geoff's father's farm. By contrast, the sunsets here in the western part of the world were, he was finding, much more sudden. The sun had fallen from the sky in mere moments the previous evening, as mountain shadows fairly raced across the valley floor, eventually sliding and hopping up the mountains on the far side of the Rim and marking the beginning of another night.

It had been two weeks since Yachem had awoken. Two weeks since this fool expedition had been decided on. Two weeks of planning and preparing. Two weeks of messengers darting up and down Citadel's hill. Two weeks for Yachem's leg to heal. Now they could delay no longer, according to Priest, and the day of departure had arrived. Daniel was still only a quarter convinced that there was anything at all beyond the Rim – old books and new strangers be damned – but he was charged with Geoff's safety and *he'd* be damned if he let anything happen to the boy – no matter how prickly Geoff was going to be. The boy – the young man – had been unusually quiet for days now, and Daniel was beginning to be concerned. He shrugged. He'd find out soon enough what was up with the lad. Maybe this would be a great adventure the likes of which the valley had never seen. That'd perk him up, likely. Maybe it would be a short trip and back to the farm by midsummer. Either way would be fine with Daniel, but maybe not with Geoff.

Whistling, he strode off to check on the donkey. If they were going to leave this morning as planned, the beast would have to be set up for a long wait – until Doctor Samuel could get word to Will and Geoff's father that it was still here – before it was taken home. As he worked, Priest and his apprentice strode out of Citadel, deep in conversation. The apprentice was staying behind – his training was nearly complete and *someone* needed to perform Priest's functions in the Valley – and was obviously getting some last-minute instruction. Within a few minutes Priest and Daniel were joined by Yachem and, eventually, Geoff. Wordlessly Priest nodded, and without further delay they set off down the hill.

Two hours later, the little expedition reached the edge of Holtom's wood. The sun was high overhead, nearly having reached its peak, and its warmth made the walk into a pleasure. Daniel was thoroughly enjoying himself, weighed down as he was by Priest's books and papers and various unidentifiable bundles. The smell of springtime, all wetness and warming earth and *life*, was in the air and the road was

Lonico

dry enough to be comfortable walking. The syncopated triple thump of Daniel's boots and stick hitting the ground set a comfortable and familiar rhythm that Daniel found to be incredibly soothing. He smiled a bit, and idly listened to Geoff and Priest as they questioned Yachem about the city.

"So you don't have any power at all?"

"No, Mr. Priest. The magi make the decisions, but they also care for the people. They are the most qualified, the most learned, and..."

"So," interrupted Geoff, "can a non-mage become a mage? If they're particularly worthy, I mean."

Yachem sounded shocked. "*No*, Mr. Geoff. Only magi may be magi. They are born to it. They are different. You'll see. A servant may gain a high place and work near to the magi, and sometimes a servant may – if he is *truly* extraordinary – be *reborn* as a mage, but a servant can *never* become a mage in this life. You might as well ask whether a fish could become a dog."

Daniel turned his attention back to the road ahead, sad that the Doctor hadn't been able to make the journey with the other four men. "Too much to do around here, and nobody to do it for me," he'd said. Forty feet or so along, a groundhog's head poked out of the grass beside the road, and disappeared hurriedly at the humans' approach. At least nature's making sense, he thought. You'd never see a groundhog chasing all over the world on a whim. A small sigh escaped Daniel, but was immediately crushed by his inherent resiliency. By the time the group rounded the next bend in the road Daniel was smiling, and again listening only to the *thump-thump thump* of his footfalls.

The clustered chimneys of Market first poked over the trees a few minutes before sundown. The valley's biggest – and only – settlement, Market was home to no fewer than a hundred people and never failed to make Daniel nervous. Many of the people who lived here had never worked on a farm at all, and there were rumours throughout the valley that there had been thefts in Market – at least two or three in the last year, according to the wildest tales. There were, of course, good people here too. The smith was a kind and competent man, as had been his father. The Inn was always clean and the innkeeper's food excellent. Still, there was something that struck Daniel as *wrong* about so many people living so far from the nearest field. Priest had insisted, however, that they needed to stop here, so here they were stopping.

Yachem was shaking his head – probably surprised at how big Market was compared to his City, Daniel thought. The 'hand clapped Yachem on the shoulder reassuringly.

"Don't worry too much, Yachem. I know it's a bit of a big place, but we'll keep an eye on you. You'll be fine." Yachem smiled in response, and shook his head again. Daniel grinned at the pale man, and together the four travelers walked into the town.

In order to minimize the amount of farmland that was eaten up by Market, the town was crowded in on itself: a dense tangle of wooden buildings and narrow streets. The countryside was lost almost immediately from view. The smells and sounds of the town were very different from the smells and sounds of the valley proper, the healthy earthen odours replaced by the musk of humanity and the stench of the shops owned by the smith and tanner. The arrival of Priest in Market – especially alongside someone so strange looking as Yachem – caused a great stir in the town, and it wasn't long before the daily life of the place had come to a crashing halt.

Yachem turned to Daniel. "Why do they stare at us so?"

Daniel nodded to a familiar face in the crowd, and replied. "Well, part of it's Priest. He never leaves Citadel except in an emergency, like for a birth or a wedding, and the people'll know that something's up. Most of it's you, though."

Yachem nodded. "I thought it might be something of that nature. We are quite a curiosity, the four of us."

"The two of you, maybe," Daniel laughed. "Geoff and me, we've been here many times before. Old hands at Market-visiting, here. Right Geoff?" Geoff merely nodded his assent before he returned to his brooding.

Before too long the group reached the doors of the Inn – a long, low building, built mainly as a place for farmers to stay if they needed to visit market and couldn't make both legs of the trip in a single day. The four men tramped in, and Daniel walked over to the innkeeper to ask about lodgings. He directed them to bunk in numbers one and

Lonico

two – none of the rooms being occupied at the moment – and offered to help carry their belongings up.

Yachem seemed surprised that Daniel didn't pay the innkeeper, and said so.

"Pay him? What?"

"Well... if you do not pay him, how is it that he can afford to operate the inn?"

Daniel thought about the question for a few minutes. "It's his job, Yachem. That's what he does. He's the innkeeper. Everyone in the valley sends part of their produce for the year to Market, and part of it to Priest and the doctor, and in return people like the smith and innkeeper and tanner do their jobs as best they can. That's how it's done."

"What if one of them wants more than they have been given? Or cheats?"

Daniel stopped walking. "Cheats? Why would they cheat their friends and family? They get enough, and we've enough to share... do people do that where you're from? Cheat?"

"All the time, Daniel. Where I'm from, unless you are a mage, people will try to cheat you. It is the way it is done."

Daniel shook his head and continued walking towards the small but comfortable rooms that the keep and his wife had made up for them. He opened the door and, after stowing his bags neatly under the bed, sat down gratefully. Yachem perched on the other bed and began to hum as he examined his boots for wear. A few minutes later, Priest knocked, and then stuck his head around the door. Yachem leapt to his feet, but Priest laughed and waved him back to his seat.

"Relax here for the evening. I need to go speak to someone, and then we'll be carrying on tomorrow morning. I think Geoff's already headed over to the square, if you want to join him."

Priest withdrew his head, shut the door gently, and walked down the hallway. His soft footfalls faded away into silence almost immediately.

Daniel closed his eyes and luxuriated in the feel of a bed under him. If he wasn't mistaken, it would be the last time in a while that he'd have a good night's rest. He was asleep before Yachem finished cleaning his boots.

8

Yachem lay awake in his bed for a long time after Priest left. For a while he considered going over to the square to find Geoff, but eventually decided against it. Geoff had never, it seemed, particularly warmed to the servant, and for his own part he could never quite do away with the first terrifying image he'd had of this strange valley. The image of Geoff's blue eyes staring down at him and *weighing* him – calculating Yachem's value against a pound of herring, or a *dok*, or… or whatever it was that constituted wealth up here – still haunted him.

Yachem wondered, not for the first time, if he should be helping these people at all. On the one hand, they seemed harmless. Daniel seemed to be a genuinely friendly – if somewhat reserved – man, and this Market of theirs was barely big enough to fill up Yachem's own tiny neighbourhood of Bridgeshadow. If this was truly their only town, they were no threat to the city of Lonico or to the magi who protected it. On the other hand, there was Priest. He certainly presented himself as a gentle, kindly man, but Yachem had heard of magi who presented a pleasant face to the world and would still strip the flesh from an insolent servant's bones in a heartbeat. There was also Geoff, with his calculating eyes. Could this all be some sort of elaborate ruse intended to get Priest and Geoff inside the City? Could they possibly be *that* dangerous? Yachem shivered despite the fire-warmth of the room. Sleep was slow in coming, and not restful when it did.

The next morning broke sooner than it felt like it should have. Yachem was awoken by Daniel's gentle prodding at his shoulder.

"Best get up, Yachem. Sun'll be up in a few minutes, and we can't have Priest thinking that we're lazing around now, can we?"

Yachem wrenched his eyes open and heaved himself upright.

Lonico

Yawning, he threw on his clothes. He was re-lacing his left boot when Geoff rapped on the door.

"Priest sent me to wake you guys up. I guess there wasn't much point in it, was there?" Yachem opened his mouth to respond, but was overrun when Geoff continued. "Come on. We're leaving as soon as we can. Priest says we're going to try to make it out of the valley by tonight – or maybe tomorrow at the latest." At this announcement, there was finally genuine enthusiasm in Geoff's voice.

Priest met them in the common area at the front of the Inn and, waving to a still sleepy and blear-eyed innkeeper, led them outside. The sun was just beginning to rise over the shingled roofs of Market, and the black silhouettes of the buildings with their tall peaked roofs seemed to lean crazily into each other, like sailors after a long night out in the Southdock. The air was silent and still, speaking of a beautiful day to come, and the smell of freshly-baked bread held temporary sway. The four men were quiet as they crossed the town, following the marginally wider street that connected Market to the great road that ran the length of the valley.

They walked on throughout the day – stopping occasionally to eat or allow Yachem and Priest to rest their aching feet. Daniel would occasionally indicate a point of interest to Yachem – here the largest wheat field in the valley, there the overgrown path that led down to the ruins of Aerie Peak on the southern Rim, there the rutted track which would take a traveler to the farm on which Daniel himself had grown up, a Son of the farm and not, he said, so different from Geoff. Yachem nodded along to these revelations, as much out of good manners as of genuine interest.

At some point in the early afternoon, the group turned left and headed along a slightly smaller road that led towards the north.

"Not much to the east of us now anyways," said Daniel, inclining his head in that direction. "Except trees, the Rim, and a few more farms. Geoff's father's place is down there – I'd hoped that we'd be able to stop in, but… if hope was eggs, as they say."

Yachem took his word for it. Daniel was proving to be a veritable fount of folk wisdom. The four men continued north, and eventually reached a sight which stopped Yachem dead in his tracks.

A river flowed across the land here and, at some point in time, somebody had thought to bridge it. The bridge was incredible. Weather and centuries had taken their tax, wearing the pale stone away and wiping clean some of the carving, but here and there detail could still be made out. Here a dolphin leapt from featureless stone, there an octopus wrapped long tentacles around a column. At the top of another of the columns perched the eroded but still visible form of a ship in full sail. One entire plinth was a perfect carving of the great light-tower of Boelthe, an ancient wonder in a dying land a hundred miles north of the City. Yachem turned to Priest, amazement plain on his face.

The willowy man smiled sadly. "According to my books, this bridge was a gift from a city called Boelthe, in commemoration of three centuries of co-operation. Other than that, I know nothing about it. Nobody else in this valley has even heard of Boelthe, of course."

Geoff spoke loudly. "These things are real?"

Yachem and Priest nodded at the same time, and Yachem answered. "Yes, of course. What did you think them to be? Fever-dreams?"

"I've never thought about what they might be – this is just the bridge. It's been here forever. It never even occurred to me that someone would have *made* it. I mean, not that I really thought about it at all."

"Well," said Priest. "Think about it now. This is your heritage, and it's one that spans a good deal more than a few forgotten miles of valley farmland. Laii was once a power in this world. One with great and powerful friends, and one with a few implacable enemies." Priest regarded Yachem for a few moments. "All gone now, of course. Now we are truly forgotten."

Priest turned away from the others and stepped out onto the graceful arch of the bridge. Yachem, Daniel, and Geoff followed after, lost in their thoughts. As Yachem crossed, the growl-roar of the river seemed to echo ever stronger in his ears, until he could scarcely hear his own footsteps. He glanced at Daniel, who smiled and leaned towards him.

Lonico

"It's the Hole," he bellowed. "It's only about a quarter of a mile to the east of us right now. Makes a right awful noise here, doesn't it? Something about the shape of the river magnifies the noise on the bridge!"

"What's the Hole?" Yachem shouted into a sudden quiet – they had reached the far side. Yachem saw Geoff smirk at him.

"Well," said Daniel, "the Hole's a whirlpool. The streams and rivers of the valley all come together in this one pool, see, and the water just sort of drains out. I'm not sure where it all goes. Out under the Rim, maybe. If you drop something in the Hole though, it's gone forever. Or if someone falls in. Happens occasionally. They've never yet found anyone who has gone down the great funnel of the thing. It's a sight worth seeing, for sure."

Yachem nodded. "It surely would be, Daniel. It surely would." He shivered at the thought. The roaring gurgle of the water filling your ears, the crush, the deadly slow drag down into the cold blackness. The stark impossibility of your spirit's journey back to the shores of the sea and the promise of rebirth.

The day wore on and the sun fell towards the mountains, still clearly visible in the west. As the group approached the northeastern corner of the valley the land started to rise. There was no tall and steep hill like the one that Citadel perched on, but the climb was perceptible, and taxing on Yachem's child-weak legs in the thin alpine air. Eventually, gulping for breath that he couldn't seem to catch no matter how many frantic breaths he took, Yachem asked for a break. Throwing himself down onto a convenient rock, Yachem sucked in great gasps of cool air and scooted around to look back the way they had come. The valley was small enough to be almost entirely visible from this vantage. It seemed still. Quiet. A patchwork of tended fields, a slight smudge of smoke over Market, and the distant black speck against the mountains that could have been Citadel were the only signs that any humans lived here at all. The only dangerous thing in this valley, thought Yachem, is the Hole.

Soon his breath was back and, feeling physically and emotionally better, Yachem fairly sprang to his feet. The rest of the walk passed quickly. As the sun reached the up-straining peaks of the western

Rim's western curve, the small party reached the northern edge of the valley. The transition between fertile valley earth and naked black rock was startlingly, unnaturally sudden. The path petered out well before the knife-edge of the rock, a knife-edge that was broken and chipped by a massive swath of tumbled stone. The scar, thousands of tons of stone ripped from the mountain, ran for hundreds of yards up the mountain's face and then disappeared over the lip of the peak. Yachem tried to imagine the kind of forces that would have been required to shift that amount of rock – to splinter the bones of the world – and failed. The cliff appeared to be completely unscaleable.

"How," asked Geoff from behind Yachem, "are we supposed to climb that?"

Yachem was wondering the same thing. There was no visible path, and he was sure that someone would have looked for ways over the Rim in the time after the cataclysmic event that had bottled up this mountain fastness. Surely, if there was a way up, someone would have found it by now.

"Someone," said Priest, "found a way up. He came to Citadel last year and told me that he'd climbed the Rimwall. I didn't believe him, at first, but he insisted. He was terrified by the experience, and that, more than anything else, convinced me that he was being truthful. I went to see him last night, and he told me how he did it. It shouldn't be too much trouble for us. He said that from the top he could see a whole other world…" Priest's voice trailed off. "We should try to find the bottom end of his path upwards this evening. We'll make the ascent tomorrow. Sleep well tonight, for tomorrow we pass beyond the world of Laii."

Lonico

9

Geoff could not follow Priest's advice that night. The thought that by tomorrow evening they'd know more about the outside world than anyone living in the valley was far too thrilling for sleep. Geoff also found, to his surprise, that he couldn't shake a deep sense of regret. Tomorrow he'd be saying farewell to the only place that he'd ever known. No matter how unfairly he'd been treated by fate – being born second was an endlessly repeated slap in the face – the valley was home. That night, as he stared up at the boughs of a fir tree silhouetted against the stars, Geoff vowed that he'd never return to the valley of his birth until he had made himself great. He would shake the world, and wouldn't his father be surprised?

And Will. Will might be a Farmer in his own right by the time Geoff got back, but Geoff would show him anyway. He'd have his own farm, somewhere, or be special – someone like the smith, or even Priest. He smiled to himself in the dark.

Soon enough, the sun started to dribble gold on the western peaks of the valley, lighting one after the other. The pattern of their illumination was intimately familiar to any valley man. First the Westheight, then the Knife, then Citadel's Peak and so on were bathed in the warming light of the sun. Geoff watched in silence for a few moments, savouring the last view of the valley he might ever have, and then began the short process of gathering his things.

By the time the other three were awake, Geoff was done and standing at the path up the cliff-face that they'd found the previous evening. A rockslide had tumbled down the mountain here, some time in the last couple of years, and it had left behind it a ragged stairway of jumbled stones that might be barely climbable. Waiting for the light of day to strike the path and allow a safe ascent was one of the hardest things that Geoff had ever had to do. Even understanding that the shifting shadows of early morning would make the climb impossibly treacherous didn't help to ease the anticipation, or dull the pain of the wait. He paced at the bottom of the trail while the others took their ease on the soft spring grass, and watched the line of sunlight ooze its way across the valley floor. He chafed as the light blazed down upon Market. He groaned as the sun picked out the Boelthan bridge, the white stone glowing suddenly in the morning. He nearly screamed as the brightness inched up the track from the valley's centre and seethed as the sun poked out from behind the peaks and picked out the first handholds of the trail to the top of the world with exquisite unhurriedness.

The four men climbed the path. Even though you sometimes had to scrabble upwards on all fours, the going was fairly easy and Geoff could tell that although the path was little-known now, it would not be so for long. One way or another, the centuries-long isolation of the valley was going to come to an end. He was still among the first, however, and he swore that he'd make his mark, no matter the cost.

The rockslide chute came to an end at the western end of a broad plateau that sat like a saddle across the spine of the mountains. Great peaks towered far above the travelers' heads on every side, but here the ground was relatively flat. Knee-high grasses and half-buried stones made the walking dangerous, though. A twisted ankle up here would be no laughing matter. Geoff kept his gaze fixed firmly on the ground before him, and allowed Priest to lead them across the plateau. That was why, when Priest stopped suddenly in front of him, Geoff was only fifty feet from the black bulk of the fortress carved into the side of the mountain. Smaller than Citadel, it was nevertheless an imposing structure. Also, Citadel was constructed of individual stones, while this building had been hacked from the rock of the mountain itself. Tiny arrow-slits gazed blankly down on the travelers, and the only visible door gaped forlornly open. Great gaping holes punctured the castle's walls at various places along the perimeter.

"Magic," said Yachem. "Only magic could have done this."

Priest nodded sharply. "This is – was – the fortress of Bastion. Last-built and smallest of the valley's citadels, it didn't stand long against your *magi*." There was a twist in the last word, Geoff noticed.

Lonico

Like it tasted sour in Priest's mouth. "It was destroyed, and its defenders slaughtered, in order that the valley might be sealed without probing eyes or interfering hands." Priest sighed and shook his head. "Come. We're working for the future. Worrying at the skeleton of a long-dead empire will do nobody any good."

Yachem and Priest walked on and, after shooting Geoff an unreadable look, so did Daniel. Geoff stared at the ruined stronghold for a few more moments and followed the others through a narrow and twisting cleft between two mountains. Every few feet, windows pierced the mountain-stone to either side of them, and ruined walls had once jutted into the pass to slow attackers. The fortress of Bastion had obviously honeycombed the rock in this area – although none of the elaborate defenses had been enough to protect it against the magi of Yachem's city. They had only walked a few hundred more paces, however, when they reached the edge of the Rim and saw the world spread out before them. A low layer of clouds – a layer of clouds that was below Geoff's feet – obscured much of the view, but here and there he could see the trees of a vast forest. He gasped. The rest of the world was huge – maybe six or even seven times the size of the valley! He looked at Daniel, who was shaking his head slowly and licking his lips, and at Priest, who was decidedly grey.

"I think," said Priest, "that I'm going to be sick." And he was. When he was recovered somewhat, he sighed. "I knew it was going to be big, but I wasn't prepared for this."

He waved his hand towards the right, a direction in which Geoff had until now completely failed to look. An ancient road snaked off steeply down the mountainside, clinging precariously to the slopes and peaks, and eventually plunging into a thick tuffet of cloud. At the top of the road, a few dozen feet to the south of the place where Geoff now stood, was a massive bridge. Or rather, the remains of a bridge. A few of the huge stones used to construct it still clung to the far side, and a pair of columns remained standing on the near edge, but only an enormous chain – a hundred feet long and with links as big as a child – still connected the two worlds.

Geoff blanched. It was immediately apparent that the four travelers were going to have to creep across the chain if they wished to continue. The crevasse that the bridge had spanned was easily a thousand feet deep, and the sides appeared to be nearly sheer. Geoff kicked a stone over the edge experimentally, and never heard it hit the ground. He heard a thump from behind him, and turned to see Yachem sitting awkwardly on the ground. Priest was still pale and looking ill, and Geoff wasn't feeling too steady himself. Only Daniel, dependable as ever, looked more or less unfazed. The 'hand then did something truly amazing.

"No sense waiting around, I guess. I'll head across first to make sure it's safe."

No sooner had Daniel finished speaking than he climbed onto the chain. With startling agility, considering that he was carrying by far the heaviest pack of the four of them, he scuttled across the links. He reached the other side safely and waved back at the other three.

"Didn't move under me," he shouted. "I reckon all three of you could come over at once and not even make it twitch!"

Geoff tightened his pack's straps. There was no way, he thought, that he was going to allow himself to be shown up by a 'hand. Until he was officially told otherwise, he was still a Son of the farm, and he'd act like it. Leaping onto the near side of the chain, Geoff raced across it on hands and feet. Long hours in the fields and woods of the valley had ensured that his grip was strong and his muscles tough, and he had no trouble crossing. He had barely put his feet on the ground on the far side of the gap, however, when a curse from Daniel and a loud shout from behind him made him spin on his heels.

Yachem was lying on the chain, grasping it tenaciously with a clenched hand and wrapped legs, and he was screaming. Priest was dangling from Yachem's outstretched right arm, swinging slightly back and forth as he strained to find some way, any way, to climb back up to the chain. Geoff's eyes widened and he sank to his knees, only vaguely aware of Daniel bellowing encouragement at Yachem.

The pale servant was still holding on. Incredibly, against all expectations, Yachem had maintained his grip on both Priest and the chain. Still, Geoff knew that it was only a matter of time before Priest was gone. Suddenly Daniel was there. Geoff hadn't even noticed the 'hand throw down his pack and take off along the swaying metal links, but he was undeniably there, sprawled on the chain next to Yachem, reaching down, clamping a brown hand around Priest's flailing wrist, yanking, pulling, tugging until all three of them were safely clutching the chain and panting above the abyss.

The three men inched their way along the chain towards Geoff. They reached the near end of the chain and hurled themselves onto the safety of the earth, where they lay gasping and shaking for several minutes. Eventually Daniel sat up.

"Well, we should probably get going then, shouldn't we?"

Yachem cuffed Daniel in the back of the head, and the three men fell about themselves, laughing. Geoff sat silently, hating his poisonous isolation.

It's them and it's me now, he thought. *A bond has been built here that I'll never share in.*

The four men made camp that night in the shadow of the bridge's ruins, too exhausted and shaken to walk any further. Talk was desultory and sporadic at first, as each of the travelers dealt in his own way with Priest's near death. Of them all, he was the unquestioned leader – the spiritual heart of the expedition, as well as of the valley. His death would have been a major catastrophe for Laii. They debated going back – getting someone else to travel with them – the Doctor, maybe. Jacob Smithson. Geoff's father. Someone. Anyone that the valley could afford to lose. Daniel was for going back. Yachem, surprisingly, for it as well. It is our duty, he said. Priest and Geoff wanted to continue onward. The valley *needed* them to continue, Priest said. If they turned back now, it might be months – years – before anyone else mustered the will to leave, said Geoff. It might be too late. Nobody else in the valley was as qualified anyway, said Priest. Only he could really hope to convince the Lonican magi to help the valley. Anyway, the hard part was over and done.

Yachem and Daniel were not immediately persuaded, but eventually their arguments were cut off. He and Priest would go on alone, Geoff said, and that settled the dispute without further discussion. As Geoff had anticipated, Daniel wouldn't abandon his charge, and Yachem wouldn't go back into the valley alone.

Geoff smiled at the darkness. He would have his chance.

Graham Angus

The next morning dawned with a suddenness that startled Geoff. Here on the eastern side of the Rim, near the peaks of the mountain range, the sun was up hours earlier than it had ever been in his life. Geoff's first real dawn was a grey and sullen thing, the sun a red boil in a pallid skein of fog, but it was still beautiful. He had never before seen the sun rise over flat ground.

The trees that had been visible the day before had faded into invisibility under the suffocating blanket of fog. Their rich green was now merely a hint of darker grey in the vaguely swirling void into which the four men descended. After a few hours of walking down the path – formerly a road but obviously long abandoned except by the occasional mountain goats who viewed the humans with stupid, startled eyes – Daniel announced that he was sure that they were below the level of the valley's floor. Somewhere above and behind us is the world we've left, thought Geoff. On the farm Will and Father are already scrabbling in the soil, reaping another crop of rocks. They're totally unaware of how much the world was changing around them – of how much it had already changed. It was all he could do to keep from giggling.

10

The path twisted its way through the mountains, working its way generally eastwards and always down, down, down. Occasionally a massive stone would jut from the short, goat-clipped grass on either side of the dirt groove in which they walked, but for the most part the monotony was unrelieved. Yachem tried hard not to concentrate on the blister growing larger and redder on the ball of his foot, but he might as well have been asked not to think about a wharf-rat chewing on his finger. He didn't recall exactly when he'd gotten soft – he sup-

Lonico

posed that it had been sometime after his former master had selected him for training as a scribe – but he knew that he had never in his life been as root-tough as these brown men of the valley. He doubted that *anyone* in the City was. These men had stout hearts, hard limbs and, apparently, feet made of cured leather. Damnation, did that foot ever hurt.

The next time they came up to one of the huge and weathered marker stones, Yachem called for a halt and sat down. He removed his boot and gingerly massaged his foot. The blister was on the verge of bursting, it seemed. Even Geoff, standing at Yachem's shoulder, grunted in what could have been sympathy when he saw the repulsive thing.

"Best poke that right away," said Daniel. "Got a needle in here somewhere."

The man started fishing around in one of the smaller pockets of his pack, and soon approached Yachem, sewing needle in hand. The servant looked away, and with a finger he traced the outline of an ancient carving cut into the stone. Such things had long since ceased to hold any wonder for Yachem – everything up here, it seemed, had been more civilized at some point in the past. Yachem clenched his jaw when Daniel lanced the blister, but in reality there was little pain and five minutes after the tiny operation was complete the foursome was moving farther down into the thick white fog.

They reached the end of the mountain road as the afternoon was giving way to the evening. The trees, previously hinted at, alluded to, between lumbering banks of low-lying cloud, erupted into view all at once as if they had been lying in wait for the travelers. The trees were massive pines oaks and maples, straining for the feeble light of the setting sun, luxuriating in the abundant moisture provided by the nearby ocean. These, thought Yachem, are ship-building trees. Yachem and his companions had obviously come down from the mountains far to the north of the city, far to the north even of the logging camps that supplied the city with its timber – hard and softwood dedicated to the service of the great ships and barges that kept the City rich.

"We are far to the north of Lonico. We must travel several days to the south before we will even get clear of this forest. We should get started," he said, and as nobody else had any better ideas that's exactly what they did.

Daniel and Geoff seemed to possess an infallible sense of direction, and Daniel would gently correct Yachem whenever he began to veer too far off course. Although Priest did his best to keep their spirits up by regaling the group with tidbits of information about the trees they passed, the group found themselves traveling in an increasingly deep silence. In the forest, where one tree looked much like another and the boughs reached out hungrily to catch every sunbeam, they all quickly lost track of the time. They walked among the great trees until the sun went down and plunged them all into a sudden darkness, deep and still. They made camp under a gigantic oak – its bole easily twenty feet across – that curved protectively over a small hollow. Despite his city upbringing, Yachem found the forest extraordinarily peaceful. It was gentle and old and lush, a blessed place in many ways. All four travelers slept well. They were awake before dawn and already walking south by the time the sun was completely up.

On the second day, they reached the river. Roiling and thundering, it coursed east towards the ocean and presented just as impenetrable a barrier. Of the few maps that Yachem had seen, most concerned themselves only with the city and its immediate environs. Only one, painted onto the western wall of the Grand Hall of Council, had even hinted at the layout of the land north of the logging-camps. Yachem remembered a river on that map, a tiny thread of blue snaking through the heart of the deep green forest, but this… this was no thread. Spumes of water leapt skywards as the torrent smashed into rocks swept clear of vegetation by a thousand thousand days of punishment. The far shore seemed as if it was miles away.

"Well," said Geoff, "there's no chain across *that*."

"We'll have to look for a bridge or a ford or a lake or something. There's a town up here somewhere. East a bit, I think." Yachem pointed down along the river's course and Priest nodded.

"Westford," he said. "Most of Citadel's maps are long gone to rot, but there's a town called Westford near the river."

Nobody suggested that the group travel to the west. Still near enough that the ground had canted to the travelers' left as they walked, the mountains loomed much larger here than they had in the tiny mountain plateau that was Priest, Daniel and Geoff's home. Under the inchoate shout of the river throbbed a deeper roar – an echoing thunder that went on and on without end and made Yachem's molars buzz in his head when he closed his mouth. The noise had been growing all morning and had made conversation difficult for a long while before the river had even been visible. Somewhere to their west, Yachem explained, was the unimaginable waterfall that fed this river, spewing forth in an unceasing torrent from the living mountains themselves. It had not taken the four men long to realize that the likely source of the water was an ever-sucking maelstrom in an otherwise isolated valley – the Hole. Geoff in particular seemed pleased by the revelation – happy to have rediscovered something forgotten for centuries, he said.

    Geoff, Priest, Yachem, and Daniel slogged through the dense foliage of the riverbank. The stunted trees clinging to the scoured rocks nearest the water had put down profusions of gnarled roots that made the footing treacherous, and the spray kicked up by the churning water turned what soil there was into heavy, slippery muck. Going was slow, and the bass rumble of the waterfall lulled them to sleep that evening – an infinite booming echo that rolled over the still miles of forest.

Graham Angus

11

Geoff dreamed that night, and hated every second of it. Deep-voiced creatures and relentless adversaries pursued him with thunderous steps through the warrens of his mind, and he came gaspingly awake long before the sun was up. He lay still for a time, staring up into the pre-dawn darkness, and then he arose.

He paced the camp for what seemed like hours before the other three finally succeeded in rousing themselves. The dawn had already suffused the forest with a pale grey-green half light and Geoff, peering upwards and searching for the few cracks in the lush leafmail of the canopy, noticed with disappointment that the sky was deeply overcast. This was apparently all they were going to get today, lightwise. They trudged through the gloaming, away from the waterfall singing its endless song at their backs. They walked on through the day, scrambling up slick stones and slipping down them. At noon, or thereabouts, they rested briefly on a rock that reached out across a deceptively still-looking pool (only a log that had – fortuitously – bounded down the river and been immediately and ruthlessly shredded in the invisible cut-currents and eddies that swirled under the surface of the pool had prevented Geoff from leaping in for a swim.) They detoured around tangled and ancient trees which spread their roots greedily around them in the thin soil of the riverbank.

As the day wore on, they reached a town in the deep forest. The trees were different here. They were smaller and more densely packed, without the great open spaces between the trunks of the mature forest, and each step taken was a matter of imposing human will on resistant thickets of twisting vines and gnarled branches. Progress slowed to a crawl. Geoff was in the lead, forcing himself through a particularly knotted tangle, when something gave way before him and he suddenly found himself lying flat on his stomach. Too surprised even to vent his frustration, he looked up and saw a building. And another. And still more and more, stretching off into the gloom of the forest. All were silent and still.

He heard a grunt behind him, and felt himself being lifted to his feet. He nodded his thanks to Daniel, and turned to look at Yachem.

The servant shrugged. "Westford, I assume," he said. "It was a town on the great road north from the city, back when we used roads. I have no idea what they do now that everything comes and goes on ship."

"I don't," said Daniel, "reckon that they do much of anything. There's nobody here."

Geoff peered around, and immediately saw the truth in Daniel's statement. The town was *too* still. It was *too* silent. Everywhere he looked, trees and shrubs were shouldering aside stone and mortar. The forest was slowly, patiently, and inexorably reclaiming Westford from humanity. Priest shook his head.

"We of the valley aren't alone in our retreat, then. Nature seems to be dragging humanity under, piece by piece, town by town."

They strode out among the buildings of the empty forgotten city, with no sound to greet them but the echoes of their own footfalls on the uneven ground. Westford was huge, at least five times the size of Market. Geoff guessed that there were nearly two hundred buildings in it, altogether, including no fewer than three forges such as the one that the valley's smith used. How, he wondered, could a town need three forges? There was barely enough metal found in the valley to keep *one* fully employed. Of course, all of the forges in Westford were empty and rusting, now – relics of another time.

"It's like we walked right out of the world of men and into the bloody afterlife," muttered Daniel, and Geoff found himself agreeing with the old 'hand. The four of them hadn't seen another soul since long before they had climbed out of the valley. Since they'd left Market there had been nothing but a procession of mountains, ruins and ancient, silent trees. It was indeed as if the travelers had walked into an endless world of ghosts. Or worse, as if they had themselves become spirits, and were even now drifting unmourned and unnoticed through a vibrant and thriving town that they couldn't see.

A human face was both the first and the last thing that they wanted to see, at that point. Especially one that was only visible for a moment before it vanished into the foliage at the edge of the clearing. Whooping and hollering, Geoff ran towards the place where he was sure he'd seen it – just for a moment, but he'd seen it. The dense underbrush was unbroken and undisturbed. There was no sign of a hidden watcher.

"Hello?" His call deadened and sank into the plant life, fading before it had gone a hundred feet. "Is anyone there?" Only the leaves, moving in time to a sudden breeze, answered him in an eerie and prolonged susurration which did nothing to lessen the increasing discomfort that he was feeling.

When Yachem grabbed him by the shoulder, Geoff almost screamed. Together and without discussion, the four men moved as quickly as they could through the ghost town of Westford, crossed the crumbling but still-sound bridge over the frothing river, and plunged back into the woods on the south side. None of them felt much like talking about the tumbledown buildings, or about the faces in the trees that came and went like lightning-bugs – quickly and inexplicably there, and then gone before you knew it.

They were being watched. That much was certain to Geoff as they hurried south the next morning. He no longer saw faces or movement in the trees, but he'd spent enough time in forests, and in this forest specifically, to know what one should sound like as he moved through it. There was a certain pattern to the birdcalls that was different since they had left Westford. The birds were giving the travelers a little more space – going silent a little sooner, staying silent a little longer. They were being shadowed, front and back. Yachem and Priest seemed happily oblivious to this, but Daniel was giving Geoff worried looks every few minutes. Geoff could do nothing but nod slightly in return and continue to walk. If it came down to a fight, he wasn't even sure that he'd know what to do. He kept a firm grip on his walking-stick, however. It was made of good-quality valley maple, and the knobbled end was surely heavy enough to lay a man out if things turned ugly.

Neither Geoff nor Daniel was overly surprised to round a bend

Lonico

in the rough and ancient road that they were following and find themselves face-to-face with a lean, hideous man in browns and greens. He was shorter than any of the four travelers, and when he smiled he showed only a few crooked and lonely-looking teeth clinging sullenly to his reddened gums. He was made more imposing, however, by the fact that he was leaning casually on the handle of a massive knife – three feet long at least, it was, and glinting coldly even in the darkness of the forest.

"Now where," said the little man, "do yer suppose that yer all's off to? Nothin' south of here but the City, and you don't want ter go there unless one of yer's a mage." He looked at each of them in turn. "None of yer's a mage, right?"

All four shook their heads quickly, and the man relaxed a bit.

"Good. So why are yer all goin' off to the City, then? Yer stupid or somethin'?"

Geoff opened his mouth to snarl a response, but was forestalled by Yachem.

"We're going to Lonico on business, of course."

"Yeah? What kind of *business*," the small man almost spat the word, "do yer all have in the City?"

"Obviously their business is none of ours, Guise, or they'd have mentioned it."

A new voice rang out across the road, and a tall woman stepped out of the trees. She smiled at the three travelers, and despite being completely unarmed and dressed in tattered clothing somehow managed to seriously unnerve Geoff.

"As long as these gentlemen agree not to mention our presence here to anyone, we shall have no quarrel with them." She turned to Yachem.

"We *can* count on your discretion, I trust?"

Yachem swallowed and nodded mutely. "Of course ma'am... we wouldn't dream of mentioning it."

The blond woman smiled then, white teeth showing all across her face.

"Good," she said. "We value our privacy, you see, and would have hated to lose it. Have a pleasant journey."

Graham Angus

She waved idly at the four befuddled travelers, and faded from view among the trees. The lean man – Guise, Geoff thought he'd been named – glared at them for a few moments before he too strode to the edge of the path and was gone.

"Good thing for us that the blonde lady came along," muttered Daniel. "Could have gotten ugly there, otherwise."

"I wonder," murmured Priest, "why they showed themselves at all. Easier by far just to stay hidden, I'd have thought."

Geoff could not help but agree. That knife of Guise's still shone in his mind. It was a weapon of war, and nothing else – something with no purpose at all beyond killing people. Anyone who carried one so casually must be very used to ending peoples' lives. The small group had been hurrying south before. Now they practically ran through the groaning, sighing gloom of the endless forest.

12

Guise sharpened his sword by the fire that night. It was his only possession of value, a family heirloom of sorts – though not one from *his* family, of course – and he treated it with the reverence it was due. He had no formal training with it – swords were almost entirely unknown outside of the ranks of the City's guard – but long years of bloody and vicious practice had given him a certain deadly skill with the weapon. He liked to say that he knew which end to put where. The firelight made the sword gleam dully – an oblong ember burning against the dark of Guise's clothing.

Satisfied with the weapon's edge, he sheathed the sword and collapsed backwards to get some sleep. He and Sheen had been following those three strangers for miles – trying to determine whether they posed a threat to what Sheen called, not without a trace of bitter

Lonico

humour, the Free People – and Guise was dead tired. Moving silently through the wood at someone else's hurried pace was an exhausting business, even for the best – and Guise counted himself as the best. He still didn't know why Sheen had let them go like that, instead of killing them like usual and going through their pockets. Didn't rightly care, either, if you got right down to it. Sheen's reasons were Sheen's reasons. If she wanted to pretend that the Free Men were more than brigands, then she was welcome to. He closed his eyes and was soon snoring lustily.

He'd barely gotten through his first dream – a nice one with a village to burn down and plenty of screaming women for the taking – when a booted toe was jammed between his ribs. Guise came immediately awake, a curse and a snarl erupting from his rotten mouth.

"What the hell yer think yer doin', idjit?" Spittle arced upwards as he demonstrated his indignation at the shape leaning over him.

"That," said a quiet voice, "will be quite enough of that, Guise."

Belatedly, Guise recognized Sheen. "Sorry 'bout that. Didn't know why anyone'd be wakin' me up at this…"

Sheen held up a hand and Guise fell silent. The melodious voice of the Free People's unquestioned and terrifying leader lilted down out of the night.

"I've been thinking about those three gentlemen that we met on the road today, Guise. I'm very much afraid that they might not reach their destination alive. Could you see to them, as a special favour to me?"

Guise sighed loudly and heaved himself unsteadily to his feet. "Yeh, sure. I'll get them through the woods alright. Don't see why we need to babysit 'em, though."

Sheen shook her head. "You misunderstand me, my friend. The woods are a dangerous place. See to them."

"Oh." Guise touched the hilt of the sword slung across his hip. "Well yer didn't have to give them such a head-start, yer daft bugger."

"I know how much you like a chase, Guise," said Sheen. Her white-toothed grin glowed briefly in the dark, and Guise smiled in spite of himself.

"That I do, Sheen. That I do."

And he was gone.

The shadows were deep and long in the forest that night. Most were still, rooted in place, swinging slowly through their moon-traced arcs. A few, the night hunters, followed their noses and ears and the ancient instructions of instinct as they skulked between the trees. One moved unerringly south. Swiftly and silently on booted feet it ran, cold steel hanging at its hip as it went.

13

Daniel was getting more and more nervous. Three days 'till the edge of the forest. That's what Yachem had said when they'd stepped off of the mountain path and first entered these cursed and endless woods. That had been nearly a week ago. Daniel couldn't remember the last time he'd seen the sun without a screen of branches and leaves blocking the view. Part of him was starting to forget that he'd ever strode across open fields, guided a plow across the face of the earth, or even slept in the cupped hand of the valley at all. He felt like all he'd ever known was the creaking brown-green murk of the forest, the stink of rotting leaves, and the sense of being surrounded by invisible eyes.

"I hate it in here," he said, and his three companions nodded glumly. None of them were built for the forest. Daniel and Geoff were farmers, Priest was a thinking-man, and Yachem was from this City – a place that Daniel was supposed to believe was even bigger than that ghost town of Westford.

Daniel stiffened. As always, he was alert even in the midst of a daydream, and something had just changed. It reminded him of the silence that had followed the little group as they were being dogged by Guise and his lady friend, but it wasn't quite the same. Subtler. Less definite. There was *something* out there, but Daniel was damned if he could figure out what, or where. Daniel tapped Geoff on the leg with his walking-stick and put a finger to an ear. Geoff blinked and cocked his head for a moment before nodding slightly. Daniel unobtrusively shifted his grip on the walking-stick, readying himself to raise and swing it in an instant, and saw Geoff doing the same thing.

Priest and Yachem had, as usual, not noticed a bloody thing and were still yammering to each other about the ways of the city, or something. Daniel allowed himself a moment of shock at his shorttemperedness before he returned his attention to the sounds of the forest.

Nearby on the right, a sparrow called cheerily. Not an alarm call, just a standard "here I am come mate with me" kind of a sound. Ahead and behind were similarly normal, but to the left everything seemed to be stilling and quieting with every step. Damn.

A few feet away, Priest saw Daniel and Geoff wheel to the left, raising their sticks defensively. All of a sudden, the 'hand was bowled over by a compact and foul-smelling missile that streaked out of the underbrush and fell among the four travelers in a rush. Silver flashed wickedly near his head and Priest raised his stick, which was immediately battered from his hands. The shock of the impact hurled Priest from his feet and suddenly he was falling backwards, watching something screech in a shining arc towards him. He heard a gurgling scream and then the back of his head hit something hard and he stared up at the gently curving and knotted branches of the oak tree above his head. They wove around and between each other, layered, layered, and layered again in a slowly waged but hard-fought war for sunlight. These trees, thought Priest, had been fighting this war – and winning it – for hundreds of years before he had even been born. He wondered if anyone else had ever died under this tree. He supposed so – the old thing must have been twenty feet tall when the valley had been sealed. Empires had risen, fallen, and would rise again over the course of this tree's life, and the soaking life-blood of humanity was nothing but an occasional nutritious treat for it. Priest opened his mouth and tried to tell Geoff everything he needed to know, but no sound came from his lips. Oh well. He was a smart boy. He'd figure it out. He'd have to, now. Priest patted a tree root conspiratorially. The tree knew what it was all about.

Everything was so very tiring, now. Moving was far too much work, so Priest lay still. Speaking was exhausting, so he stopped making the attempt. Soon even filling his lungs became a chore, so Priest decided to put that off for a while. A second later his heart twitched one last time and finally relaxed after a lifetime of labour. That which had been Priest sped off into the darkness and never again returned to the world.

14

The jolt of wood slamming into bone vibrated up Geoff's arms. Once. Twice. Again. And again. The compact man – he who had assaulted the travelers, who had hurt Daniel, and who had, unbelievably, killed Priest – was offering no further resistance. Guise lay still on the ground. Geoff drew back the stick for another blow, and Yachem caught his arm.

"Come," said the City-man. "It is done. We should tend to Daniel. And to Priest."

Geoff threw the maple branch, chosen with care and polished over a long winter by the fire, onto the still body of Guise and walked to Daniel. The 'hand, whose warning had undoubtedly saved them all, was in fairly bad shape. Guise had come out of the trees like an arrow, and although he'd only swatted Daniel with a single passing blow, the sword had bitten deeply. Daniel's left arm dangled at his shoulder, still oozing dark blood. Yachem and Geoff hurriedly bound the wound, Geoff not forgetting to spit into the bandage to protect against ill-fate, and the two helped Daniel to his feet. The three looked down at the bloodied and still form of Priest.

They were silent for a long time. Priest had been their leader, and the spokesman for the whole valley. How were they to continue to the City without him? What were they to say when they arrived? His loss was unbelievable, and quite possibly a fatal blow to the expedition.

"I guess," said Daniel eventually, gritting his teeth through the pain in his arm "we should keep on going. No sense in turning back now, is there?"

His voice contained, to Geoff's ears, a note of funereal resignation. The three men gently carried the limp body of Priest some distance from the path and placed him in a small hollow at the base of a large tree. They had no way to bury him in the root-wracked soil. The forest, said Yachem, would take him.

Returning to the overgrown roadway, the three men paused over the still and quiet body of Guise.

"Got him good then, did you?" Daniel asked. Geoff nodded.

"He knocked you over and then went after Priest like lightning. I just… hit him in the back of the head."

Daniel harrumphed. "Well," he said, "it's a fine thing for us all that you did, Geoff. No doubt about that, and no sense thinking otherwise."

Daniel kicked some dirt over Guise's face – it was the only burial he would get from the travelers – and he and Yachem began to walk south, down the road towards the City.

Geoff hesitated for a moment, bent over the body, and then followed the two at a trot. As he jogged, Guise's sword bounced awkwardly in its scabbard at his hip. It would, Geoff thought, be more useful than the cracked wooden stick lying abandoned on the ground behind him.

Yachem, predictably, didn't feel the same way. "Only the City Guardsmen carry them, Geoff. It will draw attention to you from all angles, and little of it will be friendly. It might even get you hung."

Geoff brushed aside the servant's concerns. "We need to attract attention," he said. "If we don't stand out, there's little chance that we'll be taken seriously – or listened to at all. Priest would have been able to get us noticed on his own, but with him gone we need every advantage we can dig up."

Yachem turned to Daniel, who shrugged. "Better us having one than not, right now," he muttered. "If we need to, we can always get rid of it later."

Geoff nodded at Daniel and grinned at Yachem, outwardly pleased with this small victory. Inwardly, though, a tiny spark burned his heart and a tiny hand gripped his throat. Get rid of the sword? Not likely. The sword was all that set him apart from the servants. Daniel, Yachem, and the people in the city were mere tools to be used by the great men of the world – and Geoff did not intend to become a tool.

The three travelers walked down the overgrown road toward the south. Geoff found the going difficult – between the sword tangling his legs and the lack of a walking-stick he found himself on his hands and knees more than once – and noticed that his two companions felt little inclination to slacken their pace for him. In Geoff's heart the tiny spark of rage stuttered and burned a little brighter, and the tiny hand gripped his throat a little more tightly. They walked south through the gathering shadows, made camp late, and were walking again by the time dawn broke.

The road was a little wider now, a little flatter under their feet, and Geoff found it easier to keep up with Daniel and Yachem. The trees here, he noticed, were smaller and crouched back from the road, their competition for magnificence suspended. The game here was one where insignificance and crookedness trumped height and majesty. This was a logged forest, and all three men relaxed as the sounds of industry began to replace the empty silence of the deeper woods. Soon the chocking double-thunk of axes biting into wood and the rolling rip of falling trees echoed all around them – a reassuring hymn to industry and civilization. They caught sight of human shapes in the woods near the road, but pressed on despite their curiosity. Daniel in particular wanted to stop, eager as ever to learn anything that a professional could teach him, but Yachem and Geoff

Lonico

overruled him and the trio kept walking.

"We're only two days from the city now," said Yachem. "The loggers never go more than half a day or so into the forest, and from the edge of the woods you can reach the city in one day's walk along the north road. We'll have to dodge a couple of logging wagons, but we'll be home before too long at all."

"Home," replied Daniel quietly, "has never been farther away."

Geoff agreed, and revelled in his ever-increasing distance from the valley. It's amazing what people can get used to, he thought, and how quickly. His father's farm already seemed like a vague dream, a story from somebody else's life. Market, Citadel, even Priest seemed like wisps of insubstantial vapor, tugging at him in ways that he slightly resented. The sooner they got this request of Priest's taken care of, he thought, the sooner Geoff could start carving his own life out of the world. It had not escaped him that the trio had already covered much more land than the valley possessed – and all of it was empty, utterly unused! There would be space aplenty for him to build a farm far larger than his father's. Geoff smiled as he imagined the outbuildings he'd build – he'd need more than a single 'hand to tend it all, and his sons would have farms of their own. The road unraveled under his feet.

The trees ended abruptly where the fields began. Behind the three men, row on tangled row of maples and oaks stood groaning and sighing in the late-afternoon light. Ahead of them, well-tended fields rolled gently down and away towards an endless blue expanse.

"The sea," said Yachem. "And there, beyond that headland, stands the Island City."

They were miles off, yet, and Geoff could discern nothing but the feeble gleam of stone under a blue smudge of smoke. The road was now wide and rutted and relatively well-traveled by the various carts and wagons that kept the ships of the city whole, and they walked along it as the sun was sinking behind the mountains of the Rim.

That night they slept in a ditch beside the road, and Geoff marveled at the stars, which had been so long hidden by the grasping limbs of the trees.

Graham Angus

15

The next morning, Daniel sat alone for a long while before the other two woke. The first hint of light appeared in the east at least an hour before it could properly be called day. He shook his head slightly. Beautiful, to be sure, was the roseate pink that seeped upwards into the blue-black night. Beautiful too was the sudden shattering of light on the surface of the sea when the sun crested the horizon. It was not home, though, and Daniel wished that it was. This mission of theirs had taken on a new dimension since the attack. Priest was dead, and with him had gone the group's best hope of convincing Lonico's magi to help the valley. Moreover, Priest's death was a disaster that the valley might never recover from. There was quite simply nobody to take his place, save that half-trained apprentice. He wondered if other Priests had died too young, and what knowledge had died with them.

Daniel eased his injured arm in its sling. It didn't seem to be getting any better. In fact, it felt like someone had laid a brand against his shoulder and was sawing it back and forth against the bone. He'd tried to peel off the bandages, but they seemed to be stuck. He thought, also, that it might be starting to smell a little off. He shrugged mentally. It would get better or it wouldn't. He'd survive or he wouldn't. Daniel was no fool, and he knew that it was out of his hands. Daniel watched the local farmers spread out from the tiny wooden houses perched – he guessed – on the rockiest, least fertile parts of the fields. These men, like all farmers everywhere, had undoubtedly been awake for hours, but only now was it light enough to move their animals around outdoors without risking a broken leg or worse. He watched as one man drove his plough-horse towards him and put it to work. The animal was massive, standing easily four hands higher than any draft animal in the valley, and Daniel watched appreciatively for a few

Lonico

minutes. Eventually, raising his hand in greeting and getting a nod in return, Daniel walked over to the farmer. After a few minutes of chat, both men recognized in each other a kindred spirit of sorts, and their conversation grew genial.

They continued to talk, Daniel walking beside the farmer and taking the occasional turn on the plough – it was only polite to do so – until Geoff and Yachem awoke and, eventually, joined them. The sun was at least two fingers' widths above the horizon at this point, but only Geoff seemed to be particularly eager to get on the road.

A natural pause occurred in the conversation between farmer and 'hand, and Yachem took the opportunity to ask after news from the city.

"Well," the farmer replied after a lengthy pause, "supposedly about three weeks ago one of them magi went sailing over the mountains in a giant bubble, if you'll believe it. Heard a guardsman say that he flew off to fight the Laiians." The farmer spat on the ground. "Damn filthy murderers'd deserve it, too – although I don't envy 'em their lot, with a mage coming down on top of 'em."

Daniel slumped onto a nearby tuffet, quite suddenly feeling hot and nauseous. He barely heard Yachem start to contradict the old farmer, barely noticed Geoff reach out and grasp Yachem's arm, barely saw the quickly shaken head that silenced the servant.

A small part of Daniel's mind heard Geoff explain his collapse. "He's been terrified of Laiians his entire life. It's unfortunate, but he'll come around soon." Daniel doubted it. He had never been hated before and the shock of it hit him like a rock. He lay still on the ground, staring up at the quickly brightening sky. How, he thought, are we supposed to convince these people to help us when they hate us so?

After a few moments it dawned on Daniel that this problem was Geoff's to grapple with. Until they got back to the valley, Geoff's safety was his only concern. It was up to his master's son to sort out the valley's future.

Heartened, or at least relieved, Daniel levered himself up to his feet with his good arm. The left one had slipped its sling and was hanging uselessly by his side, throbbing and burning with every heartbeat. Daniel was sure that something was wrong, but like a good 'hand, he gritted his teeth and kept his discomfort to himself. Good 'hands didn't complain, didn't question, they just *did*. That was the way of things in the valley, and Daniel would be stone-dead before he'd disgrace himself by going against the way.

Regaining his balance, Daniel nodded to the confused-looking farmer.

"Yeah, I've always hated those bastard Laiians." Daniel spat noisily on the ground for effect. "It makes me come over all funny whenever I hear about them. I get the chills, you know? Like they're staring at me from their evil mountains. Like they've reached out and put their taloned claws around my heart and they're tearing it right out of my chest. Like their vicious…"

He was warming to the subject, and would have continued except that Yachem stepped on his toe.

Geoff immediately spoke. "He'll go on for hours, if we let him. We shouldn't take up any more of your time this morning. Straight furrows and tall corn, friend."

The farmer – Daniel had never caught his name – nodded in return and wished the three men a good day, and soon they were once again walking down the gently curving road that led toward Lonico.

It was full daylight now, though the searing disc of the sun still hovered – apparently – a mere few inches above the ocean. The greatest star rose higher and higher as the three men walked, and the ink-dark shadows pooled in the valleys and ditches eventually evaporated altogether. The land here was a vast quilt of carefully groomed and tended fields that fell gently away towards the seaside. The air was redolent with the smell of grass and corn and wheat, all of it shouldering its way upward into the warm air as quickly as it possibly could. Roads meandered here and there, dotted with the occasional cart inching away from the three travelers, bearing goods towards the hungry city. Yachem, Geoff and Daniel noticed little of this, however. Their attention was fixed firmly upon the distant place towards which every road and every cart was pointed. A distant grey blur on the shore of the sea and the vague impression of needles thrusting up out of the earth was all that could be seen, but their goal was undeniably in view.

Lonico

"Home," said Yachem, and Geoff muttered something about destiny. Daniel didn't feel like it looked much like either. *Trouble*, he thought.

A few hours later, Daniel was beginning to realize how deceiving distances could be on this plain. There were no points of reference out here except for the fields and the infinite ocean and the city itself. When they had first sighted the city he had assumed that it was only a couple of hours away. Now, with the sun already past its peak and falling gently towards the mountains in the west, the three travelers were still far from the gates. The city was huge. It seemed to have been originally built on an island, a curved sickle of basalt peeking out of the sea, but had long since burst its boundaries and sprawled haphazardly onto the mainland. The island was a bristling hedgehog of a place, with fanciful towers that looked to be hundreds of feet tall looming over the much squatter mainland quarters. As they drew closer, Daniel noticed that there seemed to be a forest of sorts just to the south of the city, albeit an unhealthy one – none of the trees had much foliage that he could make out. Daniel tried hard to ignore the sight of the maddeningly endless sea beyond – the blank vastness of it threatened to unhinge him, so he stared hard at the walls spreading before him, or the carts trundling by, or the strangely dressed people swarming along on either side of him.

The road was crowded now with travelers of every description, calling out to one another in harsh voices. People on foot shuffled aside for carts piled comically high with fruits and vegetables, or clung to them until the drivers noticed and chased them off with curses and flickering whips. Everyone, Daniel noticed, had Yachem's peculiarly dark eyes and hair, although most of them were nearly as tanned as he and Geoff were. A few people cast surprised looks at Geoff's sword – and at Geoff and Daniel's eyes, but everyone let the three men pass without comment. Daniel wondered what would happen if he were to shout out loud that they came from the valley of Laii. Would the people spit on the ground as they passed? Would they flee for their lives? Would Geoff and Daniel be torn apart by a crazed mob? He'd believe any of the above, and more. Best, he thought with a private shudder, to keep it quiet for now.

The three men walked in silence. Geoff and Daniel were too shocked by the size of the city to speak – there must be easily ten times as many people in Lonico alone as in the whole valley – and Yachem was setting a faster and still faster pace, apparently eager to get home.

They smelled the city long before they entered it via the large northern road that ran parallel to the uneasy, heaving sea. When they passed through an unmanned gate into Lonico, the stench of so many people living on top of each other – shitting and living and dying in a huge pile – nearly made Daniel gag. The wide thoroughfare they were walking down cut straight through tangled warrens of houses, shopfronts and warehouses. Even in the afternoon, presumably prime working hours when good men and women should be hard at their crafts, the street thronged with people elbowing and shoving past each other. The people were dressed in all manner of clothing – from homespun wools to garishly dyed fabrics that Daniel had never seen before – and making an absolutely unbelievable din.

"Guard your possessions, friends," Yachem half yelled over the racket. "Robberies and thefts are not uncommon here, even in the daytime. I'll take you to my home, and then we'll figure out what to do from there."

It was not to be. Even as Yachem finished speaking, Daniel felt a surge in the crowd, as if it was trying to make disgorge something huge. The pressure of people moving past them grew and grew – the press of too many strangers touching him – and suddenly fell away to nothing, and Daniel found himself standing with Geoff and Yachem in an empty space in the middle of the street. Facing them was a small and very thin man, dressed in an absurdly lustrous robe that rustled gently in the breeze. Four men wearing shining metal plates on their bodies, shining metal hats on their heads, and shining metal swords at their hips flanked him. The crowd had gone dead quiet around them, watching to see what would develop. *Gophers peering at a hawk and deciding whether it's time to run*, thought Daniel. Yachem immediately knelt in the muck and filth of the street, and tugged Geoff and Daniel down to the ground beside him.

Lonico

The small man pursed his lips and looked at the three travelers. His gaze flicked quickly past Geoff's sword – obviously he considered it of small importance – but lingered on Geoff and Daniel's eyes and hair, and also on Yachem's face.

"I had a *feeling*," he said, "that walking the north road this afternoon might pay dividends." Daniel was stunned by the beauty of the man's voice. He could have listened to it all day long. It was rich and melodious – jarringly so, from such a spindly and decrepit old man. The watching crowd seemed to feel the same way. A murmur ran through it and away down the otherwise silent street.

Yachem bowed his head a little lower, and Daniel did the same. His shoulder twinged and began to burn with a sickening pain.

"Sir," began Geoff, but the man moved a skeletal hand and the young man fell silent.

"Lieutenant, these men are now my *personal* guests in the city." The voice was, if anything, more beautiful than Daniel had thought at first. "Detail two men to bring them to my audience chamber without delay. I *trust* that does not pose a problem for you, my three young friends?"

Daniel shook his head mutely as he stared at the ground as Yachem spoke from beside him. "Of course we will be happy to attend you, your Benevolence. Thank you for taking notice of us, your Benevolence."

The cadaverous man merely nodded sharply and walked past the three men. He smelled, Daniel noticed, of flowers. Flowers and another odor, something that bit at the back of Daniel's throat and made him shudder. The mage – Daniel had not a shred of doubt that the man was a mage – reached the edge of the circle of humanity that had formed in the street and walked down a rapidly widening corridor through the crowd.

Geoff let out a huge sigh and stood. "I guess," he said, "that we don't have to worry about trying to find a mage to speak to."

Yachem and Daniel stood and looked around. Two of the metal-clad men were standing beside them. One gestured irritably.

"Come on," he said. "We're a fair trot to the island, and we aren't going to be keeping *him* waiting on *your* account."

The man turned and started walking down the road towards the waterfront. Yachem, Daniel, and Geoff fell in behind him, and the other guardsman brought up the rear. The crowd parted in a reluctant wave before the shoves and shouts of the armoured man, and they soon reached the bridge.

The bridge truly was the dividing point of the city. On one side of it crouched small ramshackle houses and shops, mostly in poor repair. At the far end of the narrow straight the buildings of the island stood tall, its slender spires and towers stretching up and up into the air, seemingly raking at the very bellies of the few puffy clouds in the sky.

The bridge itself arced high into the air – pink-flecked stone supported by pillars that lanced down into the stinking waters of the sea. Daniel had, of course, never smelt the salty fishy soup of the ocean before and he quickly decided that he wasn't a huge fan of it. The bridge was deserted – empty except for the three travelers and their escort.

Daniel asked Yachem about that – the guardsmen seemed to have no objection to speech as long as the trio kept moving – and the servant replied that this bridge was for the sole use of the magi and their guests. He, himself, had never before set foot upon it. Yachem gestured to another span that crossed the straight just south of them. That one, a stumpy little utilitarian kind of a thing, was apparently reserved for the use of the servants. He didn't seem to want to elaborate, and they crossed the rest of the way in silence.

Daniel thought that the view of the city from the bridge's apex was the best yet. From there he could see down into the mainland quarter with its twisted alleys and tumbledown shacks, and he could also see the island. Manicured and meticulously tended green areas thrived among marble and stone buildings of various shapes and sizes. The layout seemed to be random at first glance, but there was a pattern – albeit one that was beyond Daniel's ability to really comprehend. There was just the sense, to his eye, that everything was right where it should be. Long buildings of a few stories curved gracefully between the bases of the towers that soared high above the city. Statues dotted the open areas. The streets, unbelievably, seemed to be paved in marble, and were a gleaming, spotless white.

As they reached the foot of the bridge and set foot on the island for the first time, Daniel saw a flash in the window of a distant tower – and a few seconds later a dull and deep roar reached his ears. Yachem and the two guardsmen shuddered, and the one ahead of Daniel spat on the ground.

"Magic," said Yachem.

"Pray that's as close as you get to it," said the guard at Daniel's shoulder.

16

Each step that Yachem took was with greater and greater trepidation. He had been to the Island many times in his life – and almost every day since his old master had selected him to be a scribe – but he had never set foot upon it without feeling a twinge of dread. Now, summoned by an unknown mage for his own inscrutable reasons, Yachem feared for his life and for his soul. The little group threaded its way southwards through the streets, past the school buildings where the young magi were taught, past grassy parks and squat, strong storehouses, between buildings from which strange-smelling smoke billowed in gouts and haughty spires hundreds of feet high. Everywhere there were magi. They walked singly or in pairs, reading or talking quietly. Nobody paid the three weary travelers and their grim escort the slightest attention. Had they been anywhere else the group of five men, three wearing swords and two obviously strangers, would have attracted comment or concern. Not here. Here they were beneath notice.

They came to a ragged halt before a large wooden door, richly inlaid with presumably precious metals and stones, and Yachem nearly collapsed. The council chambers were once a place he would have been eager to visit – they were the demesne of the magi and their most highly-placed and trusted servants. His eagerness had drained out of him. Between the two strangers at his side and the dead master moldering away in the valley of Laii behind him, Yachem would have been happy *never* to have to stand before this doorway.

The guards gestured, the doors opened, the five men entered, and Yachem was confronted with a scene of barely-controlled chaos. The Tower of the Council was immense, nearly a hundred feet across at its base, and the first story was a single mammoth room. Guards stood near the doors and dotted the walls. The ceiling arched into darkness far above their heads, and before them a vast accretion of desks lay spread across the floor. Servants scampered everywhere, dodging past and around and over each other in their hurry, running from desk to desk with vitally important (if completely arcane) scraps of information. Here, in this chamber, the bureaucracy that kept the city comfortably fed and watered thrummed along at all times. Here was where the great sugar-ships that provided the city with wealth were designed, commissioned, and dispatched to their destinations all over the world. This room was as much the foundation of the city's wealth and influence as the magi that protected it. The melee was almost indescribably beautiful to Yachem.

He only had a few moments to gawk before one of the escorts tapped him on the shoulder and pointed at a small shadowy alcove. The group stepped into it, and the guard held up three fingers, nodding to a servant standing nearby. There was a muffled crash from somewhere deep under their feet, and the clatter of tightening chains. With a sudden lurch, the floor of the alcove heaved itself skyward. Yachem, wide-eyed, sought Daniel and Geoff's gaze. He was a little relieved when they looked nearly as terrified as he himself felt. All at once, it seemed, they were plunged into darkness and it took a few seconds before Yachem realized that they were merely passing through the ceiling. He watched in silence as they passed a floor of scribes each working so quietly that Yachem could hear, even over the ever present clink-clack of chains lugging the five men upwards, their pens scratching against the surface of the vellum on which they wrote.

Lonico

They passed through the ceiling of this second floor and, when the five men emerged again into the light, they were alone. A wide hallway, paved in marble, stretched straight ahead of them for forty feet before terminating at what looked like the far wall of the tower. The hallway walls were pierced every ten feet or so by simple doors of dark wood, and they paused in front of one. The lead escort pushed it open and pointed inside.

"Wash yourselves over there, dry off with those, and change into those." Here, he pointed at some towels and finely bleached linen clothing folded neatly on a bench. "And be quick about it. No arguments, gentlemen. We'll have some servants take care of your stuff." He stepped towards the door and then turned, fixing Geoff with a stare. "And your sword stays here, farmer."

Yachem stepped eagerly into the bathing area and plunged into the scalding water – baths were a luxury for servants who didn't work closely with the magi. He tried not to think about the work involved in getting so much water – let alone *hot* water – so far up into a tower, and instead concentrated on scrubbing several weeks of accumulated grime off of his body and face. Daniel and Geoff were noticeably hesitant to hop into the large pool, but an impatient gesture from the guard encouraged them. Yachem pretended not to hear Daniel mutter about how unnatural it was to rinse good honest valley earth down some forsaken foreign drain. He relaxed against the side of the tub and closed his eyes.

Too soon, far too soon, one of the guards nudged Yachem in the shoulder with a steel-tipped boot.

"Time to get going, gentlemen. The magi don't wait for you, not in *this* city and certainly not in this tower."

The three travelers stood, dried themselves, and changed into the waiting clothing. Yachem sighed contentedly. Between the bath and the clean, civilized clothing, he could almost believe that he hadn't been walking for three straight weeks. He followed happily on the heels of the guards as he and the culture-shocked Laiians were led from the room.

Re-entering the long hallway, the party turned to the right and stopped in front of a door that looked identical to all of the others.

The guard knocked and pulled it quietly open. The room inside was beyond anything Yachem had ever seen before in his life – far outstripping even the chambers of his old master. Magnificent tapestries adorned every wall, keeping the late-spring chill (a constant issue in a city standing on the edge of the sea) from penetrating the room. The desk which dominated the space seemed to be carved out of gold-flecked marble and caught the light from the tall windows, refracting it in shards of fire around the room. There were books everywhere – not nearly as many as had been rotting away in the library at Citadel, but in far better condition. Eldritch devices perched on various surfaces around the room, casting sharp and twisted shadows on the walls nearby. Yachem suddenly became aware of the subtle but choking smell of latent magic in the air, and realized that he'd been smelling it ever since the bathing-room. The entire tower was suffused with the stench. There were three large chairs arranged before the desk, and the guards silently indicated that Yachem and his friends should seat themselves.

Time passed. And still more time. The bars of sunlight tumbling in through the window moved silently across the floor, reddened, and began to fade. Nobody spoke. The guards stood, statue-still, flanking the doorway. Yachem, David, and Geoff grew steadily more nervous. Once, Daniel opened his mouth to say something, but Yachem hurriedly shook his head and the 'hand subsided again into quiet. The protocol was always the same, and was drilled into servant children as soon as they could understand. If summoned by a mage, you followed instructions to the letter and maintained silence once in the private chambers. The day drained slowly away.

As the last of the light was fading to nothing, a silent cadre of servants entered the room. Working with grim efficiency, they touched smouldering tapers to lamps set in the walls and kindled a fire which soon cracked cheerfully away in the ornate fireplace. Yachem tried to make eye contact with one of the servants – to re-establish the common bond of fellowship that he'd been denied for so long – but she avoided his gaze. As soon as their work was completed, the servants exited the room as quietly as they had entered. For the hundredth time since he'd boarded his dead master's balloon, Yachem wondered how Taia was, and whether he'd ever see her again. He sighed and shifted in his chair.

Yachem and the valley men sat staring into the dancing fire for a few more minutes – and then the door opened. Without preamble, the cadaverous mage from the city strolled into the room. Yachem hurled himself from his chair to the ground. Geoff and Daniel followed suit, rather more slowly and without marked enthusiasm. If the mage noticed any of this, he gave no sign. He lowered himself into the massive gilt chair – almost a throne – that hulked behind his desk, and studied some thick papers that he clutched in one clawlike hand. The three travelers remained still, their foreheads pressed to the floor.

At length, Geoff cleared his throat pointedly, and the mage's eyes raked across the three men prostrate before him.

"Sit," he said, and they clambered back into their seats. He looked them over again. Yachem could feel himself squirming in the mage's sight – a worm on a hook on a line in a boat, tiny on the endless sea.

"Your names?" They answered hurriedly, the words tripping over each other in their haste.

The mage tapped his fingers on the massive stone desktop as they spoke.

"You are obviously a city man." he indicated Yachem with a single gnarled finger. "You two," he shifted his attention to Geoff and Daniel, "are not. Neither are you, though, Boelthans or Harbishans. You *certainly* aren't Hinu – so what are you?"

Daniel kept silent and shot a look toward Geoff. The Son of the farm paused for a moment before answering, and the mage smiled.

"You have nothing to worry about, young man. You will not be harmed – if you co-operate."

Geoff hesitated a moment longer, and shrugged. "We are from the mountain valley that you call Laii. We mean you no harm."

Yachem heard a muffled curse from one of the guards at the door, and the sound of steel scraping past leather as swords were drawn. The mage's sparse eyebrows curved into a pair of sharp arches and he raised a hand to forestall the incipient violence. Yachem glimpsed the brief flash of a wand nestled deep within the voluminous sleeves of the mage's robe, and his throat tightened. Next to *that*, the guards were less than nothing.

"If these men," the mage said to the trembling guard who had laid his sword alongside Daniel's neck, "wished to attempt violence, they'd have done so long before now. One of you two run along and ask mage Sush to join us. Quickly."

Yachem saw the bar of silver fire withdraw itself from his friend's throat, and heard the thud of footfalls receding into silence.

"Laiians, you say. You do not look like soulless warrior-magi to me, honestly." A sardonic smile twisted the ancient mage's face. "You look more like farmers."

Geoff began to speak, but was again silenced by an imperious gesture from the decrepit man behind the desk.

"Mage Sush will join us soon enough. She has made a more thorough study of Laiian history than anyone else still living in this city. She shall assess the truth of your… rather remarkable claim."

Behind him, the fire crackled merrily, stupidly, away.

Minutes passed and Yachem watched the moon and stars begin to shine over the city before the door once again swung open. Framed in the doorway was a tall and graceful looking woman, dressed in an ornately embroidered robe. Her eyes did not seem to be so much brown as black – chips of midnight in the pale oval of her face.

"What do you want, Valatch? I was right in the middle of something." Yachem started at the name. Valatch was the head of the Council of Magi. If the city had a single leader, it was the frail-seeming man sitting behind the marble desk.

The old man – Valatch – did not reply, but flicked a hand toward Geoff and Daniel. Mage Sush's jet eyes turned towards the two Laiians, and widened. She stepped closer and peered intently at the pair of them. Yachem was privately very thankful to be excluded from that gaze.

"Where," she gasped, "did you find these?"

Valatch smiled. "They fell into my lap, so to speak. I took a walk along the North Road early this afternoon and there they were, just strolling right down the middle of it. They are, I assume—"

"Laiians? Without a doubt." Sush nodded sharply as she spoke.

Lonico

"That hair, the height, the eyes. What do they want?"

Valatch shrugged. "I refrained from questioning them on my own. I wanted your guidance and your confirmation before I did anything of the sort."

Sush smiled – genuinely pleased at the compliment, Yachem thought. "You honour me, and demonstrate again the wisdom that makes you our greatest mind," she said. "Do you think it best that we..."

"Yes, I most assuredly do. If you would be satisfied with the older one," Valatch indicated Daniel, "I would be happy to speak with their young ringleader here. Guards – question the servant and bring me his statement. I'd like it by tomorrow morning."

Yachem found himself snatched to his feet and saw that Daniel was likewise standing. He saw the 'hand sway, totter, stagger, and then collapse with a cry, clutching his injured arm. Sush and Valatch let out a pair of nearly simultaneous cries, and a swarm of heavily armed guardsmen flooded into the room, weapons at the ready.

Valatch summarily ordered them to remove Daniel. "It appears," he said to Sush, "that you're going to have to conduct at least the first part of your interview in the infirmary."

Yachem was hustled – not dragged exactly, but there was no question of resistance even if he had been so inclined – out of the room. He was marched down the hallway and onto the same shadowed lift that he and his friends had ridden up to this floor earlier. The chains began to rattle, and the platform sank down, past the still-scratching scribes, past the still-frantic bureaucracy, past the plain but pleasant stretches of the servants' halls, and into the warrens deep inside the island's heart.

He was ushered into a small room that had never felt the sun or heard the ocean. A large guardsman, horribly scarred across the left side of his face, removed his ear from a speaking-tube that ran up and through the ceiling.

"Let's," he rumbled in a tone and volume that rattled Yachem's teeth, "talk first about how you met your friends from the Valley."

Yachem was dumped into a wooden chair.

17

The interrogation felt like it took forever. During his time in the infirmary, magi repeatedly scrubbed his wound clean (excruciatingly painful) and applied strange salves to it (worse). In the days afterwards, however, days that he spent closeted with the mage called Sush, Daniel was never mistreated. He was never deprived of food or harmed. He was never even threatened. Nobody, in fact, so much as poked his now infection-free (but still tender) arm except to test its healing. Nevertheless, he found himself telling this strange woman everything he could remember about his life before leaving the valley. Citadel, Priest, the farm, the journey – everything had come tumbling out of him, seemingly of its own volition. Sush had been polite, even friendly, and *extremely* attentive. She had been a wonderful audience and he had given her everything he could.

Now, as Daniel was marched through the winding streets of the mainland city, he felt wrung-out and ragged, like he'd had too much cider at the fall festival. He kept imagining that he saw a half-familiar face in the crowd, popping in and out of sight like the tiniest of splinters, and just as aggravating. He was hopelessly confused by the twists and turns of the city's streets. With the spires of the island at his back, there weren't any visible landmarks that he could navigate by. If he hadn't been flanked by a party of guardsmen who seemed to know where they were going, he was sure that he could have wandered for days before he got out of this labyrinth. How did people *live* like this? Crowded in amongst each other, breathing each others' fumes, treading and preying upon one another every day. Daniel ached for a field to till, for a forest to wander, for silence, for the smell of ripening fruit. Instead he was presented with twisted, filthy streets and row upon ragged row of houses.

Eventually he was brought to a halt before a house, modest as all the others but well cared-for. The leader of his steel-clad escort thumped a fist against the low door of the house. After a few moments, the door creaked open and a familiar head poked out. Daniel burst out into a wide smile, which was answered. Yachem threw the door open and stepped into the street.

"It is good to see you again, Daniel!"

"It's good to see you too, Yachem."

The guard rolled his eyes and stepped between the two men.

"Servant Yachem," he said quickly, "This visitor has been assigned to you as your guest. You will be allotted extra funds from the city treasury to offset any costs you incur. Neither you nor the visitor will be allowed to pass the city gates until mage Valatch indicates otherwise. Do you understand?"

"Yes," answered Yachem. "I'm happy to have Daniel as my guest. May I ask when we can expect our other companion?"

The guard stood silently in the street for a moment, and then leaned in closer to the two men. In an undertone, he murmured: "Your friend has drawn the attention of the Council. He's been kept for further questioning. It… it might be a while. That's all I know."

He drew himself up to his full height, nodded at Yachem and Daniel, and walked off down the street, his men fanning out on either side of him as they went.

Daniel and Yachem looked at each other.

"What," Daniel said, "do you suppose *that* means?"

Yachem shrugged. "I hope it means that the Council is considering Geoff's request for help." He shrugged again. "We'll find out when we find out. In the meantime, please come inside. There is someone I would like you to meet."

Yachem led Daniel through the doorway and into the dim interior of his home. A few oil lamps scattered around the room provided light, feeble next to the bright daylight outside, and revealed a cramped but cheerful room. A thin but cheerful looking woman, her dark hair pulled back and knotted behind her head, stood beside the low table which dominated the space. Daniel only had to glance at the expression on her face to recognize that she was Yachem's wife, and that they were very much in love. Daniel suddenly felt like an intruder.

Yachem extended his arms to his wife, and took her hands in his. "Taia, this is Daniel. He is one of the men who brought me back to you. We owe him my life."

Taia's sudden smile was enough to warm Daniel to his toes. "Please," she said. "Sit and relax – you will always be welcome in our home. Thank you for returning my husband to me."

Daniel sat eagerly. His feet and legs still ached from the walk down the mountains and across the face of the world. Sometimes he thought that they'd hurt until the day he died. The style here in the city seemed to be for everyone to have their own chair around the table instead of sharing a couple of communal benches. Daniel found it a bit off-putting, a bit distant, but comfortable.

The three of them sat and ate and talked the morning away. As the shadows shortened, Taia stood, kissed Yachem on the cheek, and excused herself.

Daniel, now feeling thoroughly at home, asked her where she was going.

A small smile answered him. "I work down southbridge way – I'm a seamstress. Fifteen *doken* a week." There was obvious pride in her voice at this last statement, and Daniel cocked his head in confusion.

Yachem filled him in. "*Doken* are our currency, here. They represent the amount of influence a servant has with the magi – they were tokens given out to indicate favour, originally. There are five *dok* to a *doken*, and ten *doh* to a *dok*. Taia's dresses are in great demand among the more highly-placed servants – and even some of the magi – so she commands a great deal of influence."

Taia jumped in. "My husband is too modest. As one who works directly with our protectors, he commands great influence as well."

Yachem's face fell. "We'll see about that, Taia. They still haven't told me who I'm going to be working for… afterwards. If anyone. We'll see."

The next morning, Daniel began seriously to worry about Geoff, and he said so.

Yachem shrugged philosophically. "The guardsman said that it could be a while. Asking impertinent questions is unlikely to bear fruit. I don't think they'll kill him, at least not before they arrest us again." He shrugged once more. "We have no real choice but to wait and see what happens."

Daniel stared at the servant, agog. "Yachem, my friend, that is the least comfortable comfort I've ever been offered."

Yachem's mouth twitched at the corner. "It is the way of Lonico," he said. "All we can do is wait, and hope, and try to keep ourselves distracted. To that end, I'd be happy to show you around the city this afternoon. There are a great many sights to see."

"That sounds fine, Yachem. When shall we leave?"

"I am not busy right now, Daniel. Are you?"

"Nothing that can't wait."

Yachem grinned at Daniel, and the two men headed outside.

The day was cool and overcast, threatening rain. Clouds the colour of stone sulked low above the city and the wind raced through the streets and alleys, tossing trash around and reeking of the cold sea. The few people on the street wore long, hooded cloaks and hurried from door to door with unabashed haste.

Despite the weather, Daniel was glad to be out of the house. Anything, he thought, was better than sitting around the table, stewing over the possible fate of Geoff. As Daniel followed Yachem through the labyrinthine streets of Lonico trying – with increasing success – to put his young charge from his mind, he marveled at how different the City and the Valley really were. Nowhere in the valley were there so many people, or so much wealth, or a person – let alone *people* – who could spend her entire life doing nothing but making pretty dresses for others to wear.

Even on this chill and sodden day, there was enough going on to keep all of Daniel's senses occupied. Here a fishmonger selling cuts from some monster from the sea. There a pair of guardsmen carrying an intricately carved and gilded box that Yachem claimed was probably full of some sort of food seasoning. There a gaggle of women chatting amiably as they sat in a massive circle, stitching together a massive sheet of thick fabric. Something called a sail, according to

Yachem. Over here, shockingly, a legless and grizzled man shouting at passersby for gifts of *doh*. Daniel wanted to ask Yachem about the man — where were his relatives, and why weren't they feeding him? — but the servant had already pushed onwards.

The riot of colours and noises and stenches began to overwhelm Daniel, and the 'hand said as much to his friend.

"Sorry Yachem, but could we find somewhere a bit quieter and rest for a while? All these people and all this noise — it's getting to me a bit — I feel like I'm being hunted, and I can't seem to shake it."

Yachem looked at him with concern, thought for a moment, and then nodded.

"Follow me. I know a place where we can see the docks in relative peace."

A few more sharp corners and cluttered lanes, a few more surprisingly deep puddles, and they stopped before a squat doorway. Inside, rough-hewn tables, scattered randomly across a straw covered floor, slowly resolved themselves from the gloom. A few men sat silently at a long, low counter that stretched across the far wall. The stink of old beer, vomit, and unwashed people made Daniel's eyes water. Yachem stomped across the floor and spoke to an unshaven and slovenly man who was leaning against the counter with one of his fingers deep in a nostril. A few low words were exchanged, and a couple of *doh* were passed across the wood. The innkeeper — for that's what he was, despite his obvious lack of interest in his customers — nodded curtly towards an opening and went back to the important business at hand.

Yachem led Daniel through the opening, and up an ancient stone stairway that led up and around and up again to a trapdoor set in the ceiling. Through that they climbed, and were suddenly in a different world. Four stories up, and the sounds and smells of the street had fallen away into nothing. Suddenly, all Daniel could smell was the salt of the ocean wind, and all he could hear was the occasional cry of a sea bird.

"It's a pretty sorry excuse for an inn," said Yachem, "but it does have a view that is unmatched on the mainland."

Daniel agreed. The two men were standing on a small platform, ringed by a low wall, and with an unobstructed view of the entire city.

Lonico

Daniel turned in place and drank it all in. To the east, the city quickly gave way to the onyx straits guarding and sheltering the island. The towers of the island itself looked oddly shortened today, and it took Daniel a moment to realize that the tops of the massive buildings that crowned the island were actually lost to view amongst the lowering clouds. To the north, the knotted streets and ways of the city stretched off into the distance. Somewhere beyond the labyrinth lay the great northern road which led to the forest and, eventually, to home.

Daniel wondered briefly if he'd ever see home again, before he abandoned the thought as foolishness. He would get home or he wouldn't. Wondering wouldn't help him, or Geoff. Daniel turned west, and immediately understood the city a little better. Beyond the bustle of the city lay a band of tilled fields that shrank into absolute insignificance before the enormous black mass that was the Rim mountains. Dark and brooding, they dominated the entire landscape to the west, despite the low cloud cover obscuring most of their bulk. Even Daniel, born and raised amongst their peaks, could understand why they instilled such dread in the Lonicans. Before them, the spires and towers of the city appeared to be foolish, childish gestures, not even worth the effort it took to erect them. The mountains mocked, it seemed to Daniel, all of the trials and struggles of humanity. Eventually the sight of the mountains overwhelmed him, and he had to turn away.

Yachem was standing by the south wall of the tower, and Daniel walked over to join him. Before them spread the strangest sight that Daniel had yet seen in this city of strange sights. A vast assortment of wooden buildings seemed to be built right on the waters of a sheltered bay. Adorned with tall spires as they were, they seemed to be made in conscious imitation of the island of the magi. While men and women swarmed all over some of these manmade islands, others were quiet. Daniel watched for a few moments, and then followed Yachem's outstretched arm with his eyes. One of the massive wooden structures was slipping quietly into view around the island. Arranged around the spires was an assortment of sheets that seemed to be bulging as they caught the cold ocean wind. As Daniel watched, agape, the sheets were lowered and folded by tiny-looking men, and the entire contraption coasted to a gentle halt before being dragged into the bay by other, smaller, floating buildings. Daniel found his voice.

"They… they're some sort of water-cart, then?"

"Yes, although we call them ships," Yachem replied. "The city's existence depends upon trade. Trade and the protection of the magi, of course. Do you see the salt-marsh to the south?"

Daniel looked. To the south of the city, the land dropped away into the sea, mostly. Here and there tiny islands and tuffetts poked their heads up out of the water. The black and still water of the marsh stretched off beyond sight to the south and the south-west. In the distance, far to the south-west, Daniel could see a tiny ship crawling towards the city. It lay low in the water, pushed down to near-sinking by the mountain of goods heaped high on its back.

"The marsh stretches for hundreds of miles to the south of us in the city," continued Yachem. "And it wraps around the southern edge of the Rim Mountains, as well. All the way to Hin. The water is only a few feet deep in most places, and so the marsh can only be crossed in flat-bottomed barges. The barges bring clove and pepper and sugar and other things from Hin to Lonico, and here we load it onto ships to be sent to Duge or Harbisha or somewhere I've never heard of. It's how the city survives. The magi make sure that everything runs smoothly, and they protect us from…"

Yachem's voice trailed off, and Daniel looked at him. "From people like me, and Geoff, and Priest? You still think we're a threat to you?"

Yachem stared out over the ships in the harbour, and the silence stretched between the men, wide and still as a mountain valley. Neither of them noticed the face that lifted to watch them from the shadow of a vegetable stall.

Lonico

18

Geoff sat in a plush chair in Valatch's office and waited for the ancient mage to arrive. The old man, Geoff had noticed, was always late for their talks. The young farmer throttled his deepening impatience and forced himself to be still. He had been meeting with Valatch every day for nearly a week. The questions, which had at first swarmed out of the mage like bees from a hive, had tapered away a few days ago and the two men tended, now, to merely chat for an hour or two each afternoon. It was pleasant enough, and Geoff had high hopes of obtaining aid for the valley – and still higher hopes of attaining a future for himself. That didn't change the fact that he hated being made to wait in complete isolation. He hadn't seen a single human other than Valatch and his guards for days. He began to tap his foot on the floor, and was idly kicking the gilded leg of the desk when the door finally opened and Valatch walked in.

As usual, he was carrying a sheaf of papers in his arms, and he threw them down unceremoniously onto the silver inlaid desk. Unusually, he flopped gracelessly down into his chair and covered his eyes briefly with a narrow and knobbled hand. He looked, Geoff thought, exhausted. When he finally recovered his composure he blinked at Geoff, shook his head, and sighed.

"Hello, my young friend," he said. The words were dragged out of Valatch one at a time. "How are you this morning?"

Geoff made a non-committal noise that the ancient mage more or less ignored.

"Good, good." Valatch's voice trailed off into nothing. "Geoff, I'm afraid… I must tell you that we have a bit of a problem. The Council is usually of a single mind as to the resolution of any issues that come up before it. This unity of purpose has been one of our greatest strengths in the wider world and, I fear, it is a strength that we have squandered. There are… cracks showing at the moment. Most of the magi support the position that we should be aiding your people. It seems obvious to the majority of us that your valley is no longer a threat to the city, and will not be for some time. Some more radical elements, however, have suggested that the city's position should be less… less helpful to Laii. They have refused to submit to the will of the council, and have indeed taken precipitous, independent action. These forces will, if left unchecked, bring serious harm to your homeland. I find myself in the awkward position of being forced, potentially, to raise my hand against my own kin." Valatch paused and took a deep breath.

"Geoff, you know – and I know – what has to be done. I have commissioned the arming of a strike force and asked for volunteers. We must travel to the valley and intercept these renegades before they… before they eradicate your people. I need your help to prevent that. Your people need your help. This is your chance to be a great hero to your valley, Geoff. Will you take it? Will you help me?"

Geoff sat mutely. This was all too much to take in at once. War? In Laii?

"They would destroy the valley?" The question sounded infantile to Geoff's own ears.

Valatch nodded. "I'm afraid so, my young friend. The faction that would grind your people underfoot sees this as an opportunity to strengthen their places in the council – and to strengthen the city's place in the world. I wish that it were not so, but… You must trust me. And you must help me."

Geoff looked out the window for a few moments. He had been miserable in Laii, to be sure, but had no desire to see it destroyed – and perhaps he could turn this situation to his own advantage. Surely the Saviour of the Valley would be an important and influential man. He turned and nodded to Valatch.

The old man smiled and stood. "Excellent. I knew that I could count upon you. Come now, Geoff. There is little time to lose. Our enemies are already abroad, and they have allies of their own. I'm sorry to say this, Geoff, but it appears that your arrival here has precipitated a civil war."

Lonico

Geoff stood and followed Valatch to the door. Outside, a cadre of guardsmen waited, along with a pale, fat mage who Geoff had never seen before. The mage nodded to Valatch and eyed Geoff speculatively.

"Everything," he said, his voice a tinkling fluting thing, tiny for such a large man, "is prepared. They're waiting for you outside the city, and they've collected the other... Laiian." The fat mage looked again at Geoff.

Valatch nodded, and the group moved down the hall to the elevator. One of the guardsmen grabbed Geoff by the arm and dragged him along, keeping him close to Valatch. They rode the strange platform down to the ground floor of the tower, and strode out into the central room. Empty. The bustling madness which had dominated this space every time Geoff had passed through was starkly absent. The guardsmen opened the massively carved doors and the whole group stepped out into the sunlight. The great green area around the tower was likewise utterly deserted, and the group hurried towards the bridge to the mainland in the midst of an eerie silence. They had almost reached the foot of the bridge when Geoff heard a shout from behind. A young mage, taller than most, was running to catch them.

"Mage Valatch," he called, "I must insist that you stop. The decision has..." He trailed off, staring at the long staff that Valatch had extended toward him.

"Not another word, traitor," snarled the old man. "Not another word."

"Traitor? Me?" The younger mage never managed a third word. Whatever he had meant to say was lost in the deafening roar and roiling black-green smoke that erupted from the end of Valatch's staff. Geoff and the guards were overcome with coughing fits and by the time their eyes had cleared, the young mage was dead – his head and shoulders separated by a distance of several significant feet.

Geoff felt the bile rise in his throat and, before he could turn his head, he vomited – a sour puddle by the still-hot corpse of the mage. One of the guardsmen sneered at him contemptuously, but Geoff noticed that more than one of the others was also looking ill. Valatch jerked his bony hand towards the bridge, and the party began the long trek over the iron sea.

19

Daniel stamped along in the wake of the lead carriage. No seat inside for him, of course – not that he had expected or even desired one. The very idea of being in an enclosed carriage, jostled along and unable to control the animals pulling it – unable, even, to see the road's bumps and dips before the contraption bounced over them – made him a bit uncomfortable. Besides, the weather was fine. The air was cool, the sun was bright, the wind was at their backs. It was a great day for a walk, even if the *reason* for the walk still made Daniel a bit leery.

Geoff had only managed to explain it in the sketchiest fashion before being swept into the velvet confines of the carriage, and none of the guardsmen Daniel had spoken with seemed to know what was going on. Geoff had mentioned some sort of conflict among the magi, some sort of danger to the valley, some sort of plan to protect it. Daniel wondered if Geoff really had any idea what was going on. Or if he even cared.

That was an unwelcome thought. Geoff had acted very strangely in the few minutes that the two men had been able to speak that morning. Distant and preoccupied. He had barely concerned himself with Daniel's wellbeing, and hadn't even *asked* about Yachem. It was worrying. Not for the first time, Daniel wished that Priest was still with them. He also wished that Yachem had been allowed to come along on this journey. The servant had seemed willing enough – eager even – but his request had been summarily denied. The whole thing made Daniel very, very nervous. There was a rock under the surface here, waiting to break the plough. Daniel wished that he could see where it was.

The day wore on and the sun sank lower, eventually dipping behind the familiar peaks of the Rim. Daniel's mind drifted over the mountains towards his home. The fields would be well-planted by now, the young animals birthed. The days would be spent watching the crops for signs of pests, cutting wood for the winter, preparing the scythes for the coming harvest. Daniel wondered how the haul would be this year. There hadn't been much rain in the spring, and even less in the summer – at least on this side of the mountains. It could be a sparse crop, and a hard winter. Especially, thought Daniel, as there would apparently be hundreds of Lonican mouths to feed.

Daniel was snapped from his reverie by the sudden call to halt. Looking around, he realized that the sun was well down. They had marched deep into the evening before he had even noticed. Daniel marveled at his own foolishness. He would have marched until dawn before he had noticed.

The guardsmen made a quick but efficient camp. Tents sprang up as if from the ground, and the smell of cooking meat quickly filled Daniel's nostrils. Wandering through the sudden city, Daniel noticed that there were many more guards posted towards the rear of the camp than there were posted forward. *Conflict amongst the magi indeed*, he thought. The guards looked worried, and conversation was muted. It tended to die off as Daniel approached the tiny knots of men scattered around the camp, so he wandered in a bubble of silence. Eventually, he decided to go find Geoff.

A few muttered questions and a few terse answers later, Daniel found himself standing before a nondescript tent near the center of camp. Clearing his throat, he threw aside the flap of fabric that served as a door. Hearing no response, he shrugged to himself and entered. Geoff was sitting on a low travel-bed. Both man and bed were covered in fine velvets and silks. At least Geoff seemed to have gotten rid of that ridiculous sword. A man in a guardsman's tunic was handing Geoff a cup full of reddish liquid. Seeing Daniel enter, Geoff waved the guardsman away. Nodding once, he disappeared through an opening in the rear wall.

Geoff looked at Daniel for a few seconds before he spoke.

"Exciting, isn't it? Frightening, too, but exciting."

"I'm not sure," answered Daniel, "that exciting is the word that I would use. What's going on here, Geoff? You spoke of a conflict, and of danger to our home, but none of it makes any sense to me. And look at you! Priest himself never had any finery like that."

Geoff glanced down at his robes and frowned, perhaps a little self-conscious now. "They aren't really finery, just traveling clothes. And why shouldn't I have nice clothing? I'm *important* now."

"Important to what, Geoff? What's happened?"

"Oh. Well, there are two groups of magi, now. The majority of them want to help the valley, but there's a group that thinks it would be easier to just… wipe us out. They're planning an invasion of the valley."

Daniel collapsed slowly into a chair as the meaning of Geoff's words unfolded in his mind.

"That's where I come in. I'm going to make sure that this group beats the invaders to our home. Nobody but us knows where the old road reaches the base of the mountains – they'll have to spend weeks or months looking for it."

Daniel nodded quietly, and then felt chilly fingernails scrape down his spine. "I can think of one other person who'd know where that road comes out of the mountains. And he's back *that* way."

Daniel jerked a thumb over his shoulder towards the city and watched Geoff's eyes widen.

20

Yachem thumped his fingers idly on the little table in his kitchen. Being off duty was tremendously boring, and it didn't look like anyone was in a tremendous hurry to resolve his situation.

Everyone was in a tremendous hurry about *something*, to be sure, but it had nothing to do with Yachem. All day, ever since that squad of harried-looking guardsmen had stormed in, collected Daniel, and stormed right back out again, the city had seemed to groan with tension. Magi hurried by in tight knots of guards, carts rumbled through the streets, strange rumours swirled, and the stench of powerful magic blanketed the town. Everyone was on edge. There were tales of mage fighting mage, of a party of magi and guards being pursued from the city… chaos seemed to have crept into everything, all at once. Yachem hoped that Taia would get home soon.

When the door creaked open, Yachem half-rose to his feet and turned to welcome home his wife. It wasn't her. Into Yachem's home stumped a familiar figure, albeit one that Yachem had never thought he'd see again.

"But," he stammered, "we left you in the forest. You're dead, so you *can't* be here. It's not possible."

"Yer left me in the forest, fer sure. Left me fer dead and stole my sword, yer and that oak root and that boy and the one I killed."

Guise pulled a long knife from somewhere in his filth-smeared clothing and pointed it meaningfully at Yachem's left eyeball. "Now, I'm gonna kill yer too, 'less yer tell me where the boy went with my sword."

Yachem swallowed. It was the only movement he trusted himself to make, with the point of the ragged knife hovering an inch from his eye. He tried to think rationally, and realized that he couldn't. There was no way to do so, this close to death. Every second was stretched out, interminable, eternal, but somehow not leaving enough time for Yachem to think.

Caught in this forever-moment, Yachem saw the door-handle turn, agonizingly slowly, saw the door swing open, heard his wife's cheerful hello.

He managed a single, whispered "No," and then Guise was across the room. The little woodsman's arms were suddenly wrapped around Taia's shoulders, and at the pale arc of her throat lay the rusty knife. Guise kicked the door closed and grinned crookedly at Yachem.

"Now I *know* you'll tell me. Yer not going to try anything funny while I've got my knife – and my stick – so close to yer lovely young wife, are yer?"

Yachem shook his head. Any thoughts of resisting or prevaricating had evaporated when his wife had entered the room. He hoped that Geoff would be able to take care of himself. He looked Taia in the eye and smiled in a way that he hoped was reassuring. She smiled back and his heart bloomed again with love for her.

"I'm not sure where Geoff is," he began. Guise's expression immediately darkened, and Yachem hurried onwards. "But there's something big going on – and I think that it has to do with his homeland up in the mountains. A large group of guardsmen and magi apparently left the city this morning, heading up towards your forest. I think Geoff is with them."

Guise thought for a moment – Yachem could actually see the man wrestling with the idea that Yachem might be telling the truth. The seconds swept them all along into an unsure future. Finally, Guise spoke.

"If yer lying..."

"I'm not."

"But if yeh are, I'm going to come back, and I'm going to do this to *you*."

A spray of blood, and by the time Taia crumpled to the floor Guise was gone. Yachem began to scream, and it wasn't long before the first guards barged through the door. They found Yachem kneeling in a pool of blood, cradling Taia's head in his hands, and sobbing.

They weren't here to investigate Taia's murder. They made that abundantly clear by stepping over her body as if it didn't exist, dragging Yachem away from her, and forming a tight phalanx around him. He fought, of course. He screamed and he struggled to get to her, but the guardsmen held him back. They were not rough, but neither were they yielding.

A disturbance at the door, and suddenly everyone bowed their heads. The tall female mage from Valatch's office – Sush, if Yachem remembered right – stepped into the room and took in the tableau with a single weeping glance. She flicked a hand, and the guards surrounding Yachem stepped away. The pale servant leapt across the room and collapsed onto his wife's body. The horror that had grown in Yachem's life since the day his master's balloon had lurched into the sky was now complete. He couched his wife's still head in his lap and realized that he'd never really be happy again. The days ahead of him stretched out into the future, bleak and unrelieved.

He was peripherally aware of the forms of the guards and of Sush hovering over him, and of the quiet questions that were darting back and forth above his head. He was also ware that he was somehow considered a suspect – it would have been laughable, had Yachem the ability to laugh.

Eventually the guards dragged him away from her and pulled him from his home. There was a large crowd gathered outside the door, curious eyes peering at the commotion. The faces of his neighbours, friends and relatives showed surprise as Yachem was marched outside and down the narrow street. When Sush appeared in his wake, the faces turned away from him, and his friends melted into the crowd. Yachem moved through the city in a bubble of shocked and angered silence, surrounded by armed men and one very dangerous woman.

He almost totally failed to absorb any of this, of course. He was more or less aware that he would be shunted into one of the innumerable and fabled cells beneath the Island, and pretty sure that he'd never leave.

He didn't care. There was no conceivable end to his suffering. He could wither away into nothing as easily in a cell as he could in his home. At least this way, he thought, the physical torture he'd endure would approach the emotional agony he felt. He tried to moan in a heartbroken and rent fashion, but the only sound which escaped his lips was a quiet whimper.

By the time he realized that he wasn't destined for the cells, his escort had already come to a halt in some sort of encampment just north of the City's gates. Yachem was shown to a tent, given food, and more or less left to his own devices. He spent his time sobbing and attempting to sleep. Rest was a long time in coming, and when he awoke he felt more alone than he ever had before.

Yachem dressed and walked slowly to the door-flap. Pulling it back, he saw a trio of guards facing him. The tallest of them, a hulking, olive-skinned Harbishan, grinned a too-white smile at Yachem.

"If you're not going to try and escape or kill yourself," he said, "could you at least have the decency to tell someone? We were up all night watching you, and you didn't try *anything*."

"It's not right," added one of his flunkies. "It's inconsiderate."

The third contented himself with spitting on Yachem's boot.

The Harbishan turned his head slightly. "Don't do that. Killer here might get angry. Wouldn't want there to be an incident, would we?"

All three guards burst out laughing – heaving guffaws that overwhelmed the early morning silence. They were interrupted by the sudden appearance of Sush, who startled all four men by clearing her throat directly behind the Harbishan.

"Is there trouble here, servant?" Her perfectly modulated voice cut through the laughter and sent it skirling uncertainly into oblivion.

Yachem had already sunk to his knees, and answered Sush from that position. "No mage. N-no problem. These men seem to th-think that I killed my wife, which *I would never do*. There was this man, named Guise, who... who's f-from the..."

Sush cut Yachem's stammered reply off with a raised eyebrow. "Time enough for that later, servant Yachem. It may well be that it doesn't matter."

"How..." began Yachem.

"Later," replied Sush, and the tone of her voice was not one that invited further questions. "Guards, bring this man to the command tent."

Then, spinning on her heel, Sush was gone. The Harbishan sighed elaborately.

"Lucky she didn't do you in right there," he opined. "Might have, when you questioned her like that."

Working quickly, the three men clamped a rusty iron collar around Yachem's neck. They bound his hands and, securing a chain to the shackle, began to lead him through the camp. All humour and bravado had gone out of them now, replaced with a cool competence that was much more intimidating to Yachem than their half-hearted bullying had been.

Lonico

The four men wended their way through the camp, an intentional jumble designed to disguise and conceal the routes to the tents of the magi at the center of it all. Down wide avenues and narrow alleys they went, past vast palatial tents and haphazardly arranged storage areas, to the heart of Lonico's military. Yachem, now more sharply focused on the present, realized that everyone they passed seemed to be right on the edge of violence. Swords hung loose in their sheathes, and the few magi that Yachem glimpsed moved in huddles.

Squeezing town a tight passageway between a latrine tent and a wagon-mounted forge, Yachem and his escort suddenly emerged into a comparatively open area. The guardsmen came to a halt and they were immediately approached by another, larger group of armed men who approached them with leveled weapons. Password and response were exchanged, and Yachem was handed over to the new group. He cast a glance over his shoulder as he was led across the dirt of the open area, and noticed that his original escort had disappeared into the maze of virtually indistinguishable tents.

Yachem was led to a large but undistinguished pavilion and – gently – pushed inside. He took one look around, and dropped to his knees with alacrity. The tent was full of magi. A voice that sounded like a complaining vulture cut through the soft murmur of conversation.

"Servant Yachem," it said. "Arise."

Yachem stood slowly, and his eyes sought the speaker. His knees trembled slightly when he realized whose voice it was. An elderly mage sat, hunched and twisted, in his chair, regarding Yachem with undisguised calculation in his odd and mismatched eyes – one blue, one brown. Sheer force of shock prevented Yachem from keeling over in a dead faint.

Samaranth was among the most influential and among the most powerful magi in the city, but that was not the reason for Yachem's near panic. In cruelty, Samaranth stood alone. His punishments were swift, sure, and utterly disproportionate to the offenses that provoked them. Even as a child Yachem had been warned that Samaranth was the most dangerous man in the city. Intervening time had done nothing to erode the mage's reputation.

Years of training finally overrode the terror that Yachem was feeling at that instant, as his body and mind prepared to instantly obey that Voice. Yachem didn't even feel his fear drain away as the servants' generations-deep conditioning took hold of him. Around him, even the other magi had fallen silent as Samaranth began to speak.

"You have been to the valley of Laii, have you, servant?"

Yachem nodded quickly. "Yes mage Samaranth, I have."

"With Mage Oltsin in his balloon contraption?"

"Yes, your benevolence."

"What," asked the voice, soft as the tide, "became of him?"

"He died, your benevolence. The balloon was swept over the Rimwall in a storm, and we crashed into a forest on the far side. Mage Oltsin was killed on impact."

"And you were succored by the Laiians, and eventually returned to the city on foot with them. For what purpose did they come?"

"They sought help, Mage Samaranth. Their population is no longer sufficient to survive. They sought settlers and trade." A murmur ran through the gathered magi at that announcement.

"So they said, servant."

"So they said, mage Samaranth."

"You recall the route you traveled? You can retrace your steps to the valley of Laii?"

"I can."

"Good. You may withdraw."

Yachem knelt briefly, and backed towards the entrance. As he edged through the opening, he heard mage Samaranth's voice echo softly across the room.

"Sush," came the horrid whisper, "you have had some dealings with this servant, have you not?"

Any response was too quiet to hear, as Yachem found himself once more blinking in the morning sunlight. A trio of guards – a different trio of guards – stood waiting for him. Silently they shackled his neck and hands, and led him back through the twists and turns of the camp to his tent.

Once the guards had left, Yachem sat and considered his interview with Samaranth. Yachem was a naturally intelligent man, even though the terrors of recent months had not given him much of an opportunity to use his brain, and he was able to draw a few conclusions. Lonico was mounting an expedition to the valley. Maybe two. If this morning's rumours were true, Geoff and Daniel might already be gone from the city. Also, between the heavily fortified camp and the actions of the magi, it was getting increasingly easy to believe that the rumours of civil war might actually be true. There had definitely been… something in the air at that meeting. A level of paranoia that was unusual even among the magi of the city. A sense of fear. Almost, maybe, of panic.

21

Geoff strode through the camp, silk robes susurrating as he went. Servants and guards leapt out of his path as he walked, and although he was aware that they usually rolled their eyes at him after he passed, they still leapt out of the way. That was all that really mattered. He was winding his way towards the central pavilion claimed by Valatch, and he was fuming.

Simple Daniel, nothing more than a 'hand with a good pair of walking boots, might have poked a fatal hole in the plan to save Laii from those who wished it harm. Yachem. How could they have forgotten about Yachem? The man had seemed harmless in the valley, alternating between gibbering in fear and injuring himself in ill-thought-out attempts at flight, but he had eyes didn't he? He had a brain of sorts. He could remember the route to Geoff's home as easily as Geoff himself could. It was a terrible oversight to have made.

Geoff shook his head, and his scowl deepened a few notches. Had he been paying attention he'd have noticed the rolling eyes of the guards give way to nervous stares and the occasional fearful swallow.

Eventually, he found his way to Valatch's gaudy tent, and waved to the mage standing guard outside. The man turned and stuck his head inside the tent. Withdrawing it, he smiled at Geoff.

"Valatch will see you."

Geoff nodded and strode past the man. Valatch was seated in a small folding chair, hunched over a sheaf of yellowed documents in a bright puddle of lamp-light. He looked up as Geoff entered, and half-rose from his seat.

"Welcome, my young friend. What can I do for you so late in such a long day?"

"I'm sorry for the interruption, mage Valatch, but it has occurred to me that we might have a problem."

Valatch stiffened and regarded Geoff, an alarmed look plastered across his face.

"Oh? What sort of problem?"

"The servant Yachem – the one who traveled to Laii – is still back there. He knows the route into the valley as well as I do. Surely my homeland's enemies will make use of him."

Valatch visibly relaxed, and even chuckled a bit before he spoke. "If that is the problem, then there is no problem. I'm sorry that you were worried, but we left Yachem behind quite intentionally. If the others have no way to find the path up the mountains, we'd be forced to wait for them there, possibly until wintertime. *That* might not be a supportable situation. No, we presume that they have already swept up Yachem, and will therefore be only a few days behind us. We simply trust in the fact that you and your servant, er…"

"Daniel."

"Daniel, thank you. We trust that you and Daniel will be motivated to guide us more swiftly and surely than Yachem will guide them, and that your two heads will do a better job than his one will."

Geoff nodded, chastened. There were obviously wheels turning within wheels, here, and many things left to learn.

Valatch continued. "It may be, of course, necessary for some few of us to remain in Laii for a time anyway, Geoff. We can hope to eradicate the splinter group of magi at the outset, but we cannot *expect* to do so. I was hoping to ask you to continue your adopted role as our liaison to your valley until such time as we can leave safely."

Geoff flushed with pleasure. "Of course," he replied. "I'd be more than happy to act in whatever capacity you wish."

Valatch smiled. "Good, good. I expected nothing less. Now, young Geoff, if you'll excuse me, I am an old man, and I need to sleep. We shall speak again tomorrow."

Geoff said his farewells and left the pavilion. The sky had darkened during his chat with Valatch. The stars splashed overhead were his only light and he tripped over several guy-wires as he searched for his tent, but he hardly noticed. He had a purpose now. He was, as he had always hoped he would be, a greater man than either his father or his brother. He could only hope that his position as liaison would allow him to demonstrate his newfound greatness in a suitably magnificent fashion.

Entering his tent, he allowed the waiting servant to turn down the sheets, and clambered into bed to dream of glory. It didn't even occur to him that the splinter group was supposed to be ahead of them, not behind.

22

Yachem, Sush, a few other magi, and a gaggle of guardsmen stood at the opening of the forest road. The signs of the hasty passage of a large number of men and animals were evident to all.

"At least," ventured one of the guards, "we won't have to cut our way through the woods."

Sush ignored him and turned to Yachem. "So we will follow this road north until we reach the ruins of Westford?"

"Yes."

"Is there anything on this road that we should be aware of?"

"There was a group of forest people who confronted us just to the south of Westford. One of them was the man I told you about. The man who…" Yachem trailed off into silence as his throat constricted and his eyes burned with tears.

Sush snarled. "You will be of no use to us if you cannot control yourself, servant. If you are of no use to us, then we will hang you for the murder that you committed. Tales of phantom hunchback forest-dwelling murderers do not interest me, do you understand? If these people even exist, they are mere brigands, and will want no part of us."

Yachem nodded, miserable and mute.

"Good then," Sush continued in a more moderate tone. "Come, Yachem, we have things to do."

The group began to walk back to the encamped remainder of the army, a quarter-mile distant across the fields. About halfway there, Sush appeared to come to a decision. She muttered quietly to the cadre of magi who walked with them. Seven heads nodded, and fourteen arms were raised in unison. A roar that nearly knocked Yachem off his feet echoed off the forest fence, and a gaggle of corpses in guardsman uniforms fell to the ground, smoking greasily.

The magi and the servant walked on in silence towards the camp. Upon their arrival there, Yachem was ordered not to discuss anything that may or may not be lurking in the forest ahead with any of the guards or servants in camp, and was dismissed for the evening. He grabbed a small loaf of fairly fresh dark bread from the food tent and wandered aimlessly through the camp, munching and thinking. Eventually, he found himself in the storage area – carts and wagons and chest and crates stuffed full of the various supplies that kept the army on the march. Finding a quiet corner, a cart stacked high with sacks of flour, he clambered to the top and lay down to rest.

Tonight, sleep came quickly but not deeply, and he awoke around midnight. These rough sacks of flour were not as comfortable as they had seemed at first, he decided as he attempted to knead a particularly uncomfortable lump out of existence. He had just flopped down onto his back again, resigned to a restless night, when he heard the unmistakable sound of stealthy – but not quite stealthy enough – movement nearby.

Then he heard someone say the word "Now" in a hushed – but not quite hushed enough – tone.

Then subtlety, silence, and the night all disappeared for a little while. The roar of the guards' magical execution had, earlier in the day, reverberated off of the trees of the forest to the north, and the force of it had shoved Yachem in the chest hard enough to make him stagger. *This* roar made the other sound like the mewling of a kitten.

Yachem had just enough time to register a massive ball of fire exploding from a guarded supply tent of some sort, before a wall of hot and foul air swept him from the top of his cart and sent him tumbling to the ground. He spun and skidded across the dirt and was slammed painfully into the wheel of another cart. All around him, shouts of surprise and terror were fading away, soon replaced by the sound of running feet and barked orders.

Amazing, he thought, how quickly they're able to recover. Great people, our masters. It's a pity that they seem to want to kill each other. A chunk of wood, hurled sharply upwards by the explosion, arced silently out of the sky and buried itself deeply in the ground a foot and a half to Yachem's left. He yelped, and rolled gracelessly under the cart. Lying curled up around his bruised shoulder he finally, incredibly, fell into a deep and dreamless sleep.

He awoke the next morning when a horse almost stepped on his head. Only some peripheral awareness on the animal's part saved him from *that* ignominious fate, and he scrambled out from under his shelter in a bit of a panic. The horse-handler was startled, to say the least. Yachem apologized to the handler – who was really no more than a boy – and hurried off.

He found Sush in an absolute fury. The mage spared him a quick glance and a nod and returned to her business, which at the moment consisted mainly of spitting out orders at a terrific rate of speed. These orders continued even as Sush stepped into a large carriage, beckoning Yachem and a few magi in after her. Once all were safely seated and the carriage began to move, the stream of instructions was spewed out the window to a group of messengers trotting alongside. As each was given his orders, he darted off into the thronging crowd.

Yachem didn't understand a great deal of what was being said, but he gathered that the events of the previous evening were officially considered to have been an accident of some sort. Yachem, of course, knew without a doubt that the explosion had *not* been an accident. He also knew, however, that the attack was the work of magi – and he didn't know which ones. To say anything at this point could very well be suicide. He looked nervously around at the magi who shared the carriage with himself and Sush. Inscrutable faces regarded him in return, and he hurriedly switched his attention to his own shoes. Who did he think he *was*, suspecting magi of such a thing? Even in the quiet of his head, it was a shocking suggestion.

The army, attenuated now and nervous, snaked into the trees and by noon was gone from the plains around Lonico. The farmers who lived along the path that both armies had taken returned to their homes – to despoiled fields and shattered, empty houses. Even an army in its own country and with its own supplies to draw on does not tread softly upon the earth. Yachem gazed out the carriage's window at the gnarled and angry trees and wondered what sort of mark these armies would leave on the forest, or whether it would would mark them first.

23

Daniel shook his head slightly as Geoff breezed by trailing a cloud of some Lonican perfume. The boy had refused to even acknowledge the 'hand's existence for the last day or so, and Daniel had more or less given up. They would be home soon enough, he supposed, and then Geoff's father would put things to rights. Daniel sighed and dropped down onto a large stump, victim of some long-ago logging expedition. He massaged his aching calves and looked at the trees that ringed the army's most recent camp.

The trees felt different this time through the forest, he thought. Whereas before they had seemed to be a smothering force pressing in on the small group at all times, in the presence of an army of humans they seemed lessened – recoiling from an invasion by an unwelcome species of exotic pest. He shook his head. Only a couple of months away from the fields and his brains were already going soft.

Daniel's idle observation of the trees was fortuitous. If he had been looking elsewhere, he'd never have noticed the slow, stealthy, but undeniably unnatural movements amongst the shadows of the great boles. He wouldn't have recognized the suddenly-visible profusion of small saplings for what they were – longbows. He couldn't possibly have had time to yelp and hurl himself into cover behind his stump before the first yard-long shaft slammed into the ground next to him.

Huddling behind the meager shelter the stump provided, Daniel cursed under his breath. How had Geoff forgotten to warn Valatch about these people?

Forty feet away, Geoff hurled himself into a roofed wagon and waited for things to resolve themselves. This, he thought, ought to put an end to Valatch's stubborn refusal to believe in the forest people. Ought to, also, increase Geoff's standing with the old mage. He smiled a pleased little smile and listened to the smack-clatter of the arrows on the metal roof. Outside, he could hear the shouts of surprise and screams of terrified pain give way to bellowed commands as the guardsmen organized themselves and streamed towards the attackers who had so suddenly appeared out of the woods.

Geoff checked the view from the various small windows puncturing the wagon's walls. Nothing. Nothing. Cloud of dust from the fight in the woods. Nothing. Daniel cowering behind a stump muttering to himself. Nothing. Nothing. A second group of green-and-beige clad archers slinking through the woods on the east side of the camp. He should tell someone about that, he thought.

He was casting about for someone to tell when he realized that it wasn't that urgent after all. The magi had seen the second group, and a group of about twenty were moving to meet them. The magi were wearing ornate leather armor over their flowing robes, and each of them was carrying one of the long warstaves that they were so fond of. Valatch had explained that while a wand was sufficient for everyday magic, serious fights required warstaves. The mage had refused to explain why, exactly, but had suggested that they allowed magic to be projected at a greater distance, or with greater force.

Geoff watched in horrified fascination as the magi hurried forward and took cover behind a low stone wall jutting out of the earth – further proof, had Geoff needed any, that this forest had once been inhabited. At some signal, several of the magi pulled fist-sized rocks from pouches slung low at their hips, waved their hands theatrically, and hurled the stones high overhead towards the still-advancing archers.

Geoff rolled his eyes. Of the ten or so thrown rocks, only one had struck a target – the rest rolled harmlessly to a halt just in front of the advancing fighters. Anyone born in Laii could have thrown better than that at the age of five. In fact, the man who had been struck was already climbing back to his feet, shaking his head but otherwise seemingly unharmed. Geoff sighed. If that was the best that the magi could do, he didn't hold out much hope for surviving the afternoon. He began to search for an escape route or, failing that, a hiding place. Consequently, he almost missed the show.

Out of the corner of one eye, he saw a plume of fire, and then another, and another. He whipped his head around, and saw a slaughter already well in progress. Green-clad bodies littered the ground outside the camp, shredded and scorched. Half were already down, and the remainder seemed to have been shocked into inaction by the sudden detonations at their feet. Then the magi began to move. Flowing over and around the low wall like an un-dammed river they swept towards their reeling attackers. Magical fire erupted from war-staves and smaller wands as the magi charged forward. It was not a fight. Nobody *could* have fought back against that. It was an extermination. Moreover, Geoff was pretty confident that this group of magi could have dealt just as easily with a group two or three times larger than the one they faced. Within moments, the attackers were dead or fleeing into the trees.

Lonico

He paid scant attention as the surviving archer oozed back into the forest and were gone, nor did he really notice the grim business of caring for the wounded and the dead. In his mind's eye, he was already kicking down the front door of his father's hovel, brandishing a warstaff.

Then, Geoff saw it. One of the magi, careless or clumsy or just frightened, had allowed his mind to wander and had left one of the magic stones lying out in the open. As yet, nobody had noticed the precious orb, nestled against the stone wall behind which the magi had taken cover.

Leaping out of the wagon's only door, Geoff worked his way through the camp toward his prize, working hard to ensure that he appeared to be moving casually and aimlessly. He needn't have bothered – nobody was paying him the slightest attention. When he picked up the stone and felt the shifting of the magic inside, noted the slight blue cast to the thing, felt the cool smoothness of it, Geoff knew that he'd taken an enormous step forward – although towards what, he didn't know. He cradled it in his hand, noting the texture. More ceramic than stone, really, perfectly round and light for its size. He shoved the globe deep into a pocket and moved back through camp.

As a sign of his particularly high spirits, he even condescended to nod to Daniel, although he wasn't sure if the 'hand even noticed, as he was hunched low over a corpse. *Probably going through the poor fellow's pockets for loose change*, he thought. *Peasants. I'm not sure why I even bother.*

Daniel finally gave up, and held the cook's hand silently as the man's heart-blood welled out of him. The arrow had punched deep into the man's chest and Daniel had known that hope was a faint thing, but he had still tried to force the blood to remain where it should. A combination of pressure on the wound and the stubbornness that gouges wheat out of mountain stone might succeed where reason and skill failed. For a moment, just for a moment, he had felt it working. The man had calmed and quieted under Daniel's hands, and his breathing had evened. The pressure of hot blood had slackened against the pressure of callused palms, and the cook had managed a feeble smile. And then he gave a shudder and a sigh and stopped moving altogether. The coursing fountain of arterial blood had died away into a mere trickle as the heart ceased its not-eternal-enough push against the bounds of the body.

He vaguely noticed Geoff swan by, serene in his frippery, and for the first time in his life Daniel didn't acknowledge the greeting of a Son of the farm.

24

In the days following the attack, the camp was even more tense than usual. Mage-led scouts swept the forest around the lumbering force at all times and the guardsmen, bearing the brunt of the work and doing the bulk of the dying in the assault, were beginning to tire. By the morning that the advance elements of the army reported that Westford was only a few miles to the north, bodies and tempers were at the breaking point.

The army pushed on through the abandoned city. Although the scouts reported that the forest was empty of people, Geoff couldn't shake the feeling that there was still a face watching at every window, and an ambush at every corner. The eerie silence and tree-infected streets tore at him as surely as a sword-thrust.

He asked Valatch what had become of the people of Westford, and the ancient mage shrugged.

"Some came Lonico, of course, but most went north to Boel-the. When a city begins to die, people tend to move towards their families, and Westford was always a mixed town. When the overland trade ended there was no reason to live here anymore, and the place just dried up."

With that the mage fell silent again, his thoughts presumably taken up by the grim spectacle of decay that rolled past the carriage window.

Lonico

A few hours later the final element of the guard strode across the wide bridge of Westford. Camp was pitched, even though the afternoon was yet young. Valatch called the magi and the guard-captains to attend him and — as nobody seemed to object — Geoff hovered at the edges of the conference and listened in.

"Captains," he began, "how are your men?"

The burly and scarred men looked nervously at each other. Eventually one of them licked his lips and spoke. "Mage Valatch, they are tired and frustrated and frightened."

Valatch nodded. "As I expected. Captains, inform your men that the magi shall patrol the perimeter and keep watch this night. The men may take their ease until sunup tomorrow — the cooks shall provide extra rations and drink. Dismissed."

The captains saluted and, smiling, left.

Valatch turned to the magi. "I'm going to need three ten-man watches, as well as some volunteers for the perimeter sweeps. I also want a strong guard over that bridge — no fewer than five magi at any time — and by tomorrow morning I'd like there to be a nice surprise in place for anyone who tries to cross the river from the south. Understood?"

The magi nodded, and began to wrangle amongst themselves. The prize assignment, Geoff gathered in the few moments he listened before slipping away, seemed to be the booby-trapping of the great bridge. It might, he thought, be worth watching that.

Geoff was shocked when, several hours later, a burly guard held up a warning hand and informed him that the bridge was strictly off-limits to all non-magi. He had become used to being left more or less to his own devices, allowed to go where he pleased without question, and the sudden restriction rankled him more than it otherwise would have. Remonstrations and veiled threats, although they made the guardsman visibly uncomfortable, got him nowhere. Eventually Geoff gave up on watching the enchantment of the bridge and stumped down the path towards camp, casting the occasional spiteful glare over his shoulder at the still-visible guard.

When he was sure that the man was out of sight, Geoff leapt from the path and waded in amongst the trees. Circling wide around the sentry he headed towards the bridge, confident in his ability to avoid detection. Geoff might not have possessed Daniel's honed skill for silent movement, but there was no way that some city guard was going to hear the soft, practiced tread of a Laii-raised man moving through the woods.

The sound of the river grew in his ears, but Geoff could still hear the call and chatter of the magi over the constant roar. He slowed almost to a crawl. As he moved, he tried to pretend that he was simply hunting rabbits back home. Intelligent rabbits. Intelligent rabbits who could kill him with a glance. Briefly, Geoff considered giving up and heading back to camp. His natural curiosity and sense of entitlement got the better of him, however, and he edged a bit farther forward.

Suddenly he could see the bridge. The five magi assigned to guard the stone structure were peering curiously down at the work going on below them. There, Geoff saw at least a dozen other magi struggling to maneuver barrels and lengths of cord and strange implements of magic into position under the bridge. One of the men below called to the men above, who hurriedly retreated to the north end of the span. The work under the bridge came to a halt, and most of the magi began to clamber up the banks of the river and congregate on the north bank. The one mage who remain below – Geoff recognized the one who had ordered the guards off of the bridge – pulled a flask of something out of his robes. The liquid in the flask shone like moonlight in the mage's hand, and sloshed thickly as he poured it into a box of some sort perched upon two barrels. The man paused, fiddled with something on the box, and edged slowly away from the contraption. He reached the top of the bank to subdued cheers from the rest of the magi and that, apparently, was that. The magi strolled up the path to the north, not even bothering to leave anyone behind to watch over the road leading south.

Geoff slunk back into camp with questions fizzing in his head and his magic stone heavy in his pocket. Magic had looked *nothing* like what he had expected. When nobody was watching, there was much less showmanship involved – and a great deal more equipment.

Lonico

The next morning the army moved on, and for two days and two nights all was silent at the bridge. On the third morning, a man in the uniform of a city guardsman rode up to the south end, took a long look around, and disappeared back in the direction from which he had come. By that afternoon, there was an army encamped on the south bank of the river.

25

"You're certain that there's no other crossing, servant Yachem?"

"I am certain that there is no other crossing between here and the mountains, mage Sush."

The mage dismissed the servant and regarded the bridge again. She wouldn't put it past Valatch to have left a trap of some sort on that bridge. This crisis had passed the point of verbal disagreement long ago, but if more mage's blood was spilled the damage might well be irreversible. The possibility of open warfare amongst the magi was not something that Sush was pleased to contemplate.

Her scout, a young and enthusiastic mage, scrambled over the crest of the river-bank to the left of the bridge and trotted towards her.

"As you thought, Sush, he's left a trembler on the far side of the bridge. One person at a time might be able to cross, if they go slowly and softly, but any more than that…" he trailed off and made a helpless gesture with his hands.

Sush cursed under her breath. She couldn't afford to have this bridge damaged – or to cast around for days looking for another crossing site. *Tremblers*, she thought. *Too much vibration and Woomf! You're the proud owner of a massive hole in the world.*

"Very well," she said. "I need three volunteers – light ones – to go across that bridge and deal with that trembler. I want them ready for anything they might find, and I want them to be very, very competent. We cannot have any mistakes."

The scout nodded and hurried towards the main camp to the south.

All this for a few square miles of half-abandoned farmland. All this because you couldn't put your personal ambitions aside and submit to the collective will of the Council.

Yachem watched as the three smallest magi he'd ever seen – one of them a girl barely out of her teens – walked with ludicrously exaggerated slowness across the bridge. The fifty-foot walk, normally a matter of seconds, stretched out to encompass minutes for each of the three. When the last of them reached the far side, the other magi – transfixed to a man on the spectacle unfolding before them – let out a collective sigh of relief. There was obviously some sort of tremendously dangerous spell on the bridge, Yachem reasoned. The tension thrummed like a taut line.

Yachem had seen the power of unrestrained magic before – every Servant had at one time or another seen a dissident's house reduced to rubble in an instant, and there had been the other night's attack – and he had no desire to see it again.

A nearby gasp and a distant clatter pulled his attention back to the present. On the far side of the river one of the magi had accidentally sent a rock bounding down the riverbank towards the footings of the bridge. Everyone on both sides of the river froze and watched as the stone bounced down the slope with unseemly enthusiasm, careening this way and that as it spun closer and closer to the stone support and – apparently – the absolute annihilation of the bridge and everything around it.

Someone shouted for everyone to duck but it was much too late. All anyone could do was watch as the stone took one last bounce, tumbled past the footing – missing it by the length of a finger – and plunged into the roiling water of the river.

For a moment, all was silent. Yachem let out a ragged breath. An elderly mage nearby collapsed, and a pair of servants rushed to attend him. The magi on the north side of the river resumed their descent of the bank. They reached the bottom and sidled carefully towards a deeply shadowed area near the bridge's support. They seemed to ooze into the darkness, and were lost from sight entirely.

The minutes crawled by. Eventually, one of the magi coalesced from out of the shadows and raised her hands triumphantly, a massive grin evident on her face even from such a distance. A great cheer went up from the attending magi – although Yachem noticed that Sush looked merely satisfied – and the crossing of the river began in earnest. By the next morning the bridge was alone again, and the forest had resumed its silent work, grinding the corpse of Westford into mulch.

The army groped its way northwest towards the mountains, lurching on late into the night and staggering back to its collective feet hours before dawn. Unspoken but palpable was the concern that Valatch and his people might gain the heights and dig in, tick-like and immovable, before Sush's forces could bring them to battle – or bring Valatch to his senses. If that were to happen, everyone knew that Valatch's scant numbers might be enough to force a protracted standoff in the hills, or even to carry the day.

Abruptly they reached the ragged western edge of the forest, trees giving way to wet black rocks and vertical cliffs and the throb of the waterfall to the south. The army turned ponderously to the north and continued to march.

26

Guard-Sergeant Pahaln scowled at the army just becoming visible in the mist to the south. He had found, over the last few days, that some trick of the geography – probably something to do with that freakish waterfall and the prevailing winds that leaped upward against the mountain wall – kept this area pretty much constantly blanketed in fog. All in all, it was probably a good thing. His squad of ten was perched on a switchback on the ancient road up the mountains. They were some hundreds of feet above the forest floor at a natural narrowing of the path that clung to the face of the stone. It was a perfect place for an ambush, and mage Valatch had not hesitated to take advantage of it. He had marched on up the mountain, leaving Pahaln and his squad behind him. Valatch had also left behind a trio of arcane objects that, he said, would make things very uncomfortable for an enemy army if any such thing happened by.

So. Better by far that said army, now approaching the base of the road down the mountains and not even bothering (Pahaln noted) to keep to the tree-line, didn't see the scanty defense left to slow its advance. Pahaln gestured his men to silence, and glanced nervously at the three blue and red orbs nestled in felt boxes near his feet. He suspected that he knew rather more about magic than he really should. He didn't suspect that the magi — or at least one of them — knew *exactly* how much Pahaln had learned about magic, and had assigned him this mission as a result. If Pahaln had to die, Valatch had reasoned, he might as well die usefully.

He turned his attention back to the force crawling towards the frayed end of the path. Any moment now, he thought, they'd notice the foot of the once-forgotten road and things would get started. Pahaln watched as one of the scouts ranging ahead of the approaching army stopped, turned, and scurried back towards the van of the army. The entire mass of humanity, guardsman blue freckled with the rich reds and purples of magi silks, shuddered to an uneven halt. More scouts filtered out of the main force and trickled forward to take a look. Yes, it was a path. Yes, it went up. No, the first scouts weren't lying or incompetent. Eventually a larger knot of people — magi, from the looks of their clothes — erupted from the army and flowed forward to see for themselves. Yes, it was a path. Yes, it went up. No, every scout in the army wasn't lying or incompetent. Pahaln rolled his eyes.

As the tiny bunch of magi milled ever closer to the base of the path, he began to smile. A few more feet, he thought, and they'd be within bowshot. The loss of the element of surprise would be well-spent if a few of these heretic magi – men and women so maddened with power that according to Valatch they had started a civil war – could be killed outright.

As much as every part of Pahaln quailed at the thought of raising a weapon against a mage, Valatch had been clear. These people were monsters, fratricidal maniacs who had tried to seize power and reduce the citizens of Lonico to slaves. Pahaln gestured, and his men raised their bows. *Just a few more feet.*

A shift in the group carried them closer to the black rock of the cliff-face, and Pahaln's men drew. Pahaln waited. *One more step, just to be sure.* The step was taken. Pahaln's hand dropped. The arrows screamed as they arced up, and out, and down, accelerating as they streaked toward the forest floor. Pahaln snatched up a bow, and began to shoot. The eleven archers had thirty-three arrows in the air before the first flight struck.

The whistling seemed to come from everywhere at once and grew quickly from a tiny sound, barely audible over the rustling of leaves and grasses, into something that filled the entire world. Yachem looked around curiously for the noise's source but saw nothing except equally-confused magi, trees, and the rocks of the mountains. He shrugged and turned back towards Sush. As his eyes slid 'round, they caught and held on a guardsman fleeing into the forest at a dead run. Nearby, another guard was pointing wildly into the sky and shouting something. Yachem moved his eyes upwards, and his heart suddenly thumped loudly in his ears.

Arrows. At least a thousand of them, by his panicked estimation. Falling from the cliff face. Screaming as they came. Yachem shouted – he never remembered quite what – and sprinted for the trees, Sush following hard on his heels. Most of the other magi were not so quick, and several of them paid dearly for it. The thunk of arrows striking turf and earth and the wetter sounds of arrows striking flesh echoed off of the forest wall. Screams followed, loud and long. Yachem hurled himself to the ground behind a tall and spreading oak. By the time the hellish howling cut off and Yachem opened his eyes, most of the magi in the command group were safely nearby.

Most, but not all. Yachem choked a bit to see the young mage from the bridge – still a girl, by rights – lying still and quiet at the foot of the cliffs. An arrow sprouted like a sapling from her throat.

Teams of guardsmen, crouching under wooden shields, hurried forwards to recover the dead and the injured. Yachem watched, fearing further disaster, but the mountains remained silent and still, apparently populated only by wind and the occasional roaming goat. Sush and the other magi engaged in some hurried discussion, and orders were relayed to the guardsmen. A phalanx of guards moved slowly towards the bottom end of the road to Laii. Shields upraised against an attack that wasn't coming, they edged up the path. For a long time only gravity resisted them.

A hundred feet or so from the first switchback (Yachem remembered well the elation he had felt when rounding that bend) the guards came to a sudden halt. A flash of movement from further up the path was followed by a moment of absolute stillness. Then, in silence, an explosion sent a dozen guards spinning off the path to certain death and staggered the rest of the formation. The crump of the explosion reached Yachem's ears just before the first guardsman hit the ground with an awful wet thud. Yachem heard Sush curse – a phrase more suited to a sailor fresh from Harbisha than a powerful mage, he thought – and saw her gesture wildly, snarling orders.

A troop of magi scrambled forward, protected by shield-toting guards, and began the long climb up the path. Yachem saw another explosion bloom amongst the uppermost party of guards, a hot red flower in a field of men, and more buckled and crumpled and fell.

Pahaln's men crouched nervously on either side of him as he watched the cadre of magi moving up the path, and then turned to survey the carnage caused by the two blue orbs. They had certainly worked as advertised, gouging huge chunks out of the path and the men on it. Pahaln looked at the lone red orb at his feet, the one that Valatch had ordered him to save for last. The troop of magi was closer, now. Pahaln thought that he had maybe thirty seconds. He made his decision.

"Run, boys."

His men turned as one and looked at him. One of them cocked a bushy eyebrow.

"Run. Get up the path and tell mage Valatch that we carried out his orders. I'll cover your retreat with this." Pahaln hefted the red orb.

One of the men nodded and clapped the guard-sergeant on the shoulder. "We'll save supper for you."

Pahaln tried to smile, failed utterly, and waved the men away. The ten guards scrambled up the path, and were soon lost to sight among the stones. By the time they were gone, Pahaln's attention was fixed on the still-advancing magi. For the fourth time that day he silently urged his enemies to come closer. He crouched behind a large stone and cradled the red orb in his hand. It was, he thought, maybe a bit heavier than the blue orbs had been. He'd have to wait an extra second or two to make sure that his throw covered the distance. He peeked around the edge of the stone and saw the magi, toting their warstaves and moving inexorably closer. He ducked back into his hiding place. A slow count to thirty, and Pahaln judged that the time was right. He peered around the stone again. His arm snapped back, and then forward, and the orb sailed through the air. Pahaln turned and ran. He had taken ten steps before a second sun rose right behind him.

Yachem gaped at the fireball that erupted into sudden life on the mountainside. He had seen a man break from cover and run up the path and then… white light screamed into the world. The guards on the path, the running man, the magi, all were swept away as if crushed by the fist of God. As if they had never been. The conflagration ebbed slowly but there remained an angry purple scar in Yachem's vision, which faded only reluctantly into black. Yachem discovered that he was weeping. There was something disturbingly beautiful about what he had just seen, about the lobes of light and the grey striations and the crackling sizzling boom that had accompanied it. Something about the way the very earth had shuddered before the power of the magi. Yachem retched and vomited on the fog-damp grass.

27

At the top of the mountains, standing at the edge of the deep crevasse that months ago had almost claimed his life, Daniel watched the engineers do their work. The mountain air felt extraordinarily cool and fresh after the lowland soup he'd been floundering through since this expedition had begun, and he'd forgotten how beautiful the grey of the mountains was against the blue curve of the sky. He watched a team of engineers scurrying along the massive rusting chain that linked the valley to the outside world. It seemed so long ago now that he'd left, but Daniel was almost home. He only wished that it was in better company. These magi were not acting out of the goodness of their hearts, no matter what Geoff claimed.

Trouble was about to descend on Laii, and Daniel was coming with it. It was a hard thing. Still, he was home, and he was sure that Geoff's father and the other valley men would soon see these magi off. Except that he wasn't sure about that at all. The magic of these outsiders was a terrifying force, from what little he had seen, and deep down in his bowels he knew that there weren't enough men in the valley to do much of anything about this lowland host. Daniel wasn't even sure that they'd be able to keep everyone fed through winter, if it came to that.

The bridge unfolded section by section, creeping along the massive chain in fits and starts. Daniel was having a hard time containing his mounting excitement, and his mounting dread. Across this chasm lay the valley. The bridge was getting near to completion now, and then they'd be heading home.

Maybe it was time to find Geoff. Daniel stumped off towards the command tents. Surely the boy will come to his senses and put aside this city-bred foolishness for good now that we're home, he thought.

Lonico

Surely the magi don't have so great a hold on him that he'd betray everything he was raised to stand for.

A final section of buttressed wood was heaved forward on breaking backs and slotted into place, and the engineers collapsed, exhausted. Immediately, guards and magi began to stream across the gap, and for the second time in its history the valley's rim felt the leather of a hostile army's boots.

"—and then twist like so, and we have a primed and ready war-staff. You can only use it thrice before you'll have to repeat the priming, but between it and a few other tricks I shall show you, you'll be well on the way to successfully resolving any little disputes that might crop up. As you can tell, there's a great deal more magic in the preparation than in the execution. You'll do well to remember that, and to be careful not to leave any primed staves lying around where they can be found. It would be most unwise to allow an enemy access to one."

Geoff nodded at Valatch's words. He could easily see how that would be the case. He hefted the war-staff and felt a surge of power course through his guts. Just touching this thing made him feel like he was invincible. The silk of his robe rustled as he shuddered with pleasure.

"As for the other things – orb-making, tremblers, levelers and so on – they'll have to wait. The bridge must be nearly complete, and we have many things to discuss before we move into your former home."

Geoff considered the magic stone secreted in his pocket – orb *was* a much better term for it – and tried to restrain a smile.

The ancient mage paused and his eyes transfixed Geoff, holding him like a beetle on a pin. When he spoke again, his voice was quite different. Commanding – and pleading.

"Before I continue, I must be absolutely sure of your loyalties. Absolutely sure, you understand, that you are with us – that you are one of us. I must be sure that you are willing to put aside your former life utterly and irrevocably. We can make you great, if you are with us. I will give you power over men and women, riches beyond belief, and the companionship of your true equals. I can teach you how to pluck at the very fabric of the universe and twist it to meet your needs. You can bring your valley into the wider world as a wealthy and contented place, and have fame across the planet, but *I must know that you are with us.*"

The mage stopped speaking and regarded Geoff. Everything was, for a moment, absolutely still and silent. Geoff was sure that if he pulled back the flap and looked outside, at this instant he would not see a bustling military camp, but only mountains and grass. He pulled his mind back to the present. This was, he knew, the most important question that he'd ever been asked, and he was under no illusions as to what would happen if he answered wrong.

Did he want to be a rich and powerful mage? *Yes.* Did he owe the valley anything? *No.* Did he want to show his father and brother who was really the greater man? *Oh yes indeed.* Was he with Valatch?

"Yes. I'm with you."

The mage flashed his knowing, yellow smile. "Excellent. I rather thought you might be."

Geoff smiled back, and luxuriated in the tingle running up from his stomach, out along his shoulders and down his arms. He had taken another step, he knew, towards his goal of greatness. Everything had come together, finally, in his favour. He suppressed the sudden urge to giggle like a child.

Eventually the rushing sensation dissipated and Geoff pulled himself together. He looked across the table that squatted in the middle of the tent, and saw Valatch looking back, an expression of open appraisal smeared across his face.

"There has been," croaked the mage, "a change of plans. Events down the mountain have caught up with us. An envoy – a trusted man named Pahaln – was left behind us, instructed to attempt some sort of compromise with those who would exterminate your family and friends. The emissary and his bodyguards have been slaughtered, and our enemy approaches us even now. The option of a peaceful resolution, the option I so greatly desired, has been lost to us. Originally I had intended to simply bring your people back into contact with the world, on their terms. Now, we are going to have to be more permanently involved."

Geoff sucked in a quick breath. "But that means…"

"Yes," nodded Valatch. "There will be war, and it is possible that we will never again return to the city of Lonico."

"So then, Laii—"

"—Will be our home, Geoff. The opportunity to simply leave peacefully has been denied to us by treachery. Have you yourself not said, many times, that the valley is dying? That its system of governance is unfair and inefficient? Between the two of us, and with the help of our magi and guards, we can make the valley of Laii a force beyond the ken of the worms in Lonico. We shall rule this valley as kings, Geoff, side by side and invincible. The fools in the valley need a strong hand – *your* strong hand – to rule them. There is no turning back now, Geoff. No choice but to reach out and take everything you've ever wanted. Your father and brother derided a younger son, but soon they will kneel before a crowned mage-king!"

Geoff's mouth dropped open. The plan was so different now. Everything had changed, was upside-down and perverted, but… King. *Mage*-King. Geoff quite liked the sound of that. How small his ambitions had been, mere weeks ago. How much he had grown, since. He had hoped for a farm all of his own. For the respect of his father. For the damned donkey to walk faster. That donkey was going to pay, he thought, and the ludicrousness of the idea made him shake with laughter.

He nodded to Valatch. "What, then, do we need to do first?"

In that instant, the tent's flap was flung aside and Daniel entered, fire in his eyes. The world began to change then, moment by drawn-out moment. Daniel was shouting, somewhere at a great distance, accusing Geoff of abandoning his people and his home, of being a jumped-up fool, and a patsy, and of allowing the magi to use him utterly. Geoff realized that Daniel had him by the shoulders and was shaking him, but it all seemed to be happening so very far away. All of the indignations of Geoff's life – his useless brother Will, his father, Geoff being forced off of the farm, having to tend to Daniel as they walked halfway across the world and back, dealing with the 'hand's smugness and superiority – they all leapt into sharp focus in Geoff's mind, as time slowed to near-immobility.

Across a vast and dark space, Geoff saw his arms come up to shove the old farmhand away. With agonizing slowness the scene continued to unfold – Daniel staggering back, grabbing at the tent's central support for balance, and screaming silently at Geoff. Geoff who, all of a sudden, found himself pointing the charged warstaff at Daniel. And then a flash of deepest blue and a sound like every thunderstorm in the world and Daniel stopped yelling and lay down very quiet.

And then Valatch spoke, slowly.

"So you are one of us now, and truly there is no return for you."

Geoff nodded as he looked down on the body of one of the people who had been there when he was born, and who had taught him to ride, and hunt, and walk softly on the valley floor. Now I am one of them indeed, thought Geoff. Why have I never felt less like I belong?

"I'd never have thought that Daniel would stoop to eavesdropping." It was all he could think to say.

Valatch merely shrugged in response, something unknowable dancing deep in his eyes.

28

Will strode out into the fields early that morning, and tried not to think about his problems. The sun was just blooming over the Rim as he walked towards it, into the cornfield. Will's father had noticed some weeds coming up at the east end, and Will wanted to have a go at them. There was also the matter of that footsore sheep to attend to, and Geoff's shed was falling over. Again.

As he ambled towards the rising sun, hoe slung over his shoulder, Will wondered where Geoff was. Somewhere beyond the Rim, according to his father. Will shrugged. Anything was possible, he supposed. That odd stranger certainly hadn't come from Market. Will arrived at the east end of the field and spied the tangle of weeds his father had mentioned. Leechweed. It'd suck the goodness right out of the soil if he didn't tackle it. No more time for idle musings, he thought, and went to work on the tough greenery.

The day didn't leave much time for thought or self-pity, even with the weather holding fine and the backbreak of harvest still a month off. His hoe struck a stone that morning and the entire blade snapped off of the shaft, which had meant an extra hour in the field repairing the silly thing. He'd have to get another one from the smith before harvest. The sheep weren't in bad shape though, and the shed, although impossible to fully repair on his own, would stand up until Geoff and Daniel got back. So there was that. By the time the sun began to roll down into the west, every muscle in Will's body was aching. That was the way of things, for a valley farmer.

Though there was not much time for thought during the workday, Will had all the time in the world as he slumped by the hearth that night, exhausted. By all that was holy, he missed Daniel's quiet competence. It was even possible, he thought, that he was starting to miss Geoff. Although his younger brother had often been grouchy and usually sullen, he had still been an extra pair of hands around the place. Clumsy and weak hands, maybe, but hands nonetheless. And even Will had to admit that Geoff was always quick with an idea to make the work easier. To lose him at the same time as they'd lost Daniel was a hard knock, especially with father taking the turn that he had. Hopefully both men would be home from their adventure by the time harvest rolled around, or Will would have to ask the men at Jon's farm for help. He'd never hear the end of that.

He looked over at his father, dozing on the bed. The decline in his health over the last couple of months was truly shocking. The coughing fits had finally passed as summer reached its peak, and the series of mounting fevers seemed to have ended, but Benjamin was now a brittle shell of a man. He spent most of his time in bed, eating barely enough food to sustain a six-year-old child. The old man – and he *was* an old man now – turned over in his sleep and sighed.

Outside his window a cricket chirped madly, the sound seeming to echo in the silence of the evening, and Will smiled. Everything would work itself out. If he had to ask Jon for help in the harvest, then so be it. Helping was what neighbors did. Will couldn't change the fact that his brother and their 'hand were away. Anyway, they were off with *Priest*, for the love of winter apples. If that didn't make their absence legitimate then nothing would. His father would, hopefully, get better. If he didn't, well, he had lived a good and happy life. Troubles were like cricket-song, Will decided. They expanded to fill the available space.

Contented with this thought, he ate a cold supper and turned in for the night. The sun would come up much sooner than he wanted, if he was awake much after it set.

29

The body had been stripped and draped across a rock, and had obviously been lying in the open for a few days. There was a hastily scrawled note pinned directly to the bloating flesh of corpse's chest. "The Price of Treachery." Most of the force edging up the twisting mountain path had already passed it by. Passed it and dismissed it – such things were merely weapons in the wars men fought. Even Yachem, groggy from a long night spent drawing maps of the valley and its approach, almost walked past the pathetic thing. At the last moment, however, he stopped and took another look. His heart leapt into his throat and he let loose a tiny yowl of rage and sorrow.

Sush, in conference with mage Samaranth just ahead of Yachem, swiveled in her saddle and regarded the servant.

"What," she asked, "is it *now?*"

Yachem gestured helplessly at the corpse on the rock. "It's one of the valley men. It's Daniel."

Lonico

Sush and Samaranth reined in their horses and came back for a closer look. Samaranth raised one caterpillar of an eyebrow at his colleague, and Sush nodded. She motioned a mage forward to take a look at the body.

Long, tense minutes went by as the army continued to flow noisily past the tiny island of people, and the young mage inspected the corpse. Eventually he stood, sweaty and pale, and gave a tight smile.

"It's alright. Just a body." Yachem thought that he had a beautiful voice.

The volunteer hopped down from the rock, and Sush shouted in sudden alarm. The young mage – Yachem thought his name might be Sarhon – put his foot down on a tuffet, and there was a gout of fire followed by the most incredible sound, like water ripping. Sarhon's face registered something – surprise, maybe – and then he was gone.

Yachem found himself on the ground, breathing in commingled stinks of mountain grass, blood, and magic. He felt a burning in his cheek, and raised a hand. His fingers acted of their own accord and picked out a sliver of ceramic, still hot to the touch, buried in his face an inch below his right eye. He looked at it, bloody and reeking of sorcery, as it lay in his hand. It seemed to glare evilly up at him in the afternoon sun.

"Someone buried an orb right there by the rock." Sush's voice was a little shaky, to Yachem's ears.

"Indeed." Yachem turned to see mage Samaranth rising to his feet. "And did it well, too. I was fairly sure that young Sarhon would not notice it."

Sush's jaw fell open. "You *knew* it was there?"

"Of course. Don't look so shocked, Sush. The weak are simply being seined from the school. It is a necessary process if we are to prevail. It will leave those who remain stronger. Smarter. Angrier."

The cadaverous mage turned towards Yachem. "You counted this valley man a friend, did you not, servant?"

Yachem bowed. "Yes, mage Samaranth."

"And your feelings about his murder? At his defilement?"

"Anger, mage Samaranth. At those who would do this to a good man."

"Then we shall take the body with us and bury him in the land of his birth."

Sush and Samaranth walked away then, deep in conversation. Yachem caught only part of it before they were out of earshot.

"Take what victories you can, Sush. That servant may be useful after…" Samaranth's voice was swallowed by the crowd.

A group of servants hurried forward and, carefully skirting the sticky puddle that was the remains of mage Sarhon, lifted Daniel from the rock and carried him toward the dead-cart struggling up the mountain behind the main force.

Yachem watched them go, something weak and fitful clawing at his throat the whole time. He coughed quietly, and was surprised to find himself crying. His life was emptying out. Like a barge in from Hin, his cargo was removed piece by piece. The lot of a servant – the accepted and willingly shouldered lot – was to give to the magi in return for protection. Yachem wasn't, however, feeling all that well protected right now, and he didn't have anything more to give.

Thinking of Daniel and Taia, Yachem sat down in the churned mud of the road and waited for night to hide him.

30

The Meet had been called, not for Citadel as was customary, nor even for Market which would at least have been sensible, but for a field right on the eastern edge of Laii. When he heard, Will had merely shrugged. A Meet was a Meet, no matter where you were. There were still a couple of weeks before he'd have to start worrying about the harvest, so now was as good a time as any to take a trip. Anyway, he hoped that this Meet might have something to do with

Lonico

Geoff. Maybe he'd have some help with the harvest after all. At the very least he could get a new hoe from the smith, so the trip wouldn't be a complete waste of time.

Will and his father set out the next morning. The late-summer air was already cooling, and Will checked repeatedly that the blanket remained snugly wrapped around the old farmer's shoulders. It had taken a few tries to explain the Meet to Benjamin — never mind the fact that he must have been to twenty in his long life — and Will wasn't sure just how much his father understood of their errand, even now. The old man was, however, smiling benignly from his perch at the top of the tiny cart, and Will imagined that he noticed a bit of fire returning to his father's eyes, and a bit of steel to his posture.

After the pair had met up with a few people on the road and were traveling in a loose herd of Laiians, Will was sure that his brother was back. All the talk was on the subject. Geoff had returned from beyond the Rim. Of Priest and Daniel and the stranger named Yachem — all four of the figures had loomed large in the Valley's gossip and chatter this summer — there were a dozen conflicting stories, but most people held that Geoff was not alone. Some even maintained that he had brought more strangers with him. Will and his father soon found themselves to be minor celebrities of a sort. People started asking their opinions on issues ranging from the harvest to life beyond the Rim (as if Geoff's experiences had somehow winged their way across the miles to his family). Will found himself enjoying the attention, and noticed that his father was reveling in it.

The unusual — unprecedented — procession swelled as it wound its way along the valley's ancient roads, and it soon became obvious that most of the people of Laii were in it. Will looked back as his little cart crested the white bridge, and was startled to see that there was an enormous human snake trailing along behind him. There must be almost two thousand people back there, he thought. The number was staggering. This would be, without a doubt, the greatest Meet of his lifetime.

The snake wriggled and slithered noisily eastward, and suddenly they were there. A broad field, ringed by good mountain pine, stretched for a few hundred feet before ending abruptly at the sheer black face of the eastern Rim. The field appeared to be empty. A collective shrug rippled through the crowd, and people immediately set about preparing for the Meet. Eventually, whoever had called this assembly would get things started, but there was a lot to take care of beforehand. Will pitched in with gusto, of course, and was busy rolling a gigantic barrel of ale towards the makeshift bar when he noticed a change in the sounds around him. Looking up from his task, he saw face after face pointing to the east. Following the gazes, Will saw the reason for the sudden stoppage. The golden sun of the late afternoon had picked out movement on the Rim itself.

A line of people was moving down a path cut into the face of the rock. Splotches of blue and slashes of silver, and one or two spots of red and pink were working their way towards the floor of the valley. The crowd was still now, and silent. After a few minutes, the group reached level ground and drew to a halt. The blue and silver splotches resolved themselves into nine or ten men who made up for their comparative lack of height with an extreme broadness and strength of shoulder. The two men in pink and red strolled a few feet in front of the blues, and stopped. There was a moment of stillness, and then the valley people flowed as one toward the strangers. Will found himself in a clump near the front with Doctor Samuel, the smith, and his father.

All was once again quiet, as two worlds gazed at each other across thirty feet of waving grass. Eventually, one of the strangers stepped forward and spoke, and when he did, Will recoiled in shock.

"As I promised, so have I returned," said Geoff.

Will's father's head jerked up at the sound of his youngest son's voice, and the old man tottered forward.

"Geoff? Geoff, you're back!" He got no farther before he was intercepted by one of the large men in blue and returned, firmly, to the main group.

Will gaped at the man who had been his brother. Gone were the ruddy tan and sensible, hardwearing clothes that marked every Laiian. Gone and replaced by the silk-draped pallor of this tall and slightly paunchy man. Gone too was the petulant dissatisfied twist, ever-present on Geoff's mouth. The expression of this new man was of triumph and pleasure. For the first time in his life, Will found himself afraid of his brother.

Will stared, entranced and revolted. A sudden and nervous stir through the crowd failed to pull his attention from the horror that was his little brother all grown up.

The silk-robed old man beside Geoff gestured expansively.

"As you can see," he said, "things here in your Valley are changing quickly, as too are they in the greater world. When this young man came to us he was a peasant, a scratcher of soil. In him, though, we recognized greatness. We have made him our King, and in his wisdom he has consented to become your ruler also. A great danger approaches your home now, people of Laii, and only through the strength of your King shall you be delivered!"

Will wasn't sure what a King was, but the Doctor seemed to know. The gigantic but gentle man seemed to expand suddenly as every muscle in his body tensed. Samuel strode forward, anger plain on his face.

"A King?" The Doctor's bellow echoed hollowly off the cliff-face as he approached the cadre of bodyguards encircling Geoff and his companion. "A *King?* The people of this valley haven't had a King in two hundred years, and we don't intend to let some jumped-up young—"

The wizened man at Geoff's shoulder gestured and a great boom, like a tree collapsing in a storm, echoed madly around the clearing. A woman in the front of the crowd screeched and crumpled to the earth. Geoff's eyes widened and then narrowed, and *he* gestured twice. More thumps dented the air, more eerie flashes of fire sprayed out and vanished, and Samuel staggered. He raised his hands to his chest and looked down at something he clutched in them.

"Magic," he muttered. "Ha!"

Then he toppled to the ground, and in moments he was utterly still.

Will coughed, his eyes tearing from shock and grief, and an acrid smell that seemed to be everywhere all at once. He looked blearily around, and at last noticed what had caused that stir in the crowd, earlier. On either side of the meadow, the woods had vomited out more grim-faced men and women in blue – and pale people in brightly coloured silks. They stood, silent and forbidding, for all that they looked like birds in their finery.

Geoff looked down at the prone form of the Doctor. He shook his head – a bit sadly, Will thought – and spoke.

"I wish it hadn't come to that, but we cannot – *will not* – tolerate treasonous words or actions."

The decrepit mage nodded.

"Delegate some of the best of you to come to us tomorrow and hear the thoughts and warnings of your King. We do not have much time before an enemy beyond your comprehension descends upon you, and you must be prepared for them if you are to survive.

"For now, we will be content with your oaths of loyalty. On your knees, Laiians, and swear fealty to the King of Laii; Defender of the Passes; Lord of Citadel, Bastion, and Aerie; Geoffroi the first!"

And even Will knelt, for lack of any other option, and for fear of the crackling death that his brother held in his fist. And he stumbled through an oath that he didn't understand, but – like the good man he was – he would feel obliged to honour. And the Doctor's blue eyes stared up at the depthless summer sky.

31

Geoffroi, King of Laii; Defender of the Passes; Lord of Citadel, Bastion, and Aerie, watched the small delegation of Laiians shuffle nervously into the command tent. Geoffroi sought to catch the eye of his brother Will, standing awkwardly in the first row of delegates, but was unsuccessful. All of the valley men were turned out in their finest garb. Judging from that, and from their truculent expressions, someone had taken the time to impress the importance of Kingship upon them. They would have to be cowed or co-opted – or killed. Quickly.

The scouts along the Rimwall had, that morning, reported that the second magi army, led by Sush and Samaranth, had retreated down the mountain road. There they would presumably dig in and wait for their reinforcements to arrive. If this internal dissension with the valley people was not resolved in a matter of days – a week at the most – and Valatch's magi freed to concentrate on the approaching army, Laii's defenses would likely be shattered and Samaranth would butcher them all. Valatch had been very clear on that point. Thoughts of his adviser pulled Geoffroi's mind back to the present, and he regarded the Valleymen with renewed intensity.

He waited for the shambolic horde to drift to a stop in front of the temporary throne and then nodded to Valatch. It was, as the old mage had said, time for the bait. Of course, the valley folk had already seen the hook – the Doctor's death was hardly a subtle gesture – but with any luck they'd still snap it up. Hopefully they'd realize that they really didn't have a choice. None of us do, thought Geoffroi.

Valatch hobbled forward, leaning on a primed warstaff – *how long will it be before I don't have to carry one of* those *with me*, Geoffroi wondered – and began to speak in a voice heavy with fatigue.

"Gentlemen. What we told you before is the undiluted truth. There are those in my home who have been raised and trained to believe that the men and women of the valley of Laii are bloodthirsty monsters who care not for their fellow humans and delight in the pain of others. To them, you are the shadow at the edge of sight, the stealers of children, the creep of mold on the grain. They think that you're responsible for every bad thing in the world, and that you've been hiding here, safe in your valley at the top of the world, waiting for the perfect opportunity to murder and enslave us all."

There was a brief rustle of movement as the delegates digested these words. Geoffroi imagined that they were feeling much the way that he had when he'd heard the same story: shock, disbelief, contempt, and a certain amount of pride.

Valatch, of course, had anticipated this reaction, and continued.

"So feared are you, men of the Valley of Laii, that when my people discovered that your mountain fastness had been breached by our brave King and his unfortunate compatriots, some of them resolved to kill you all.

"All?" The question was barked, derisively, from someone at the back of the knot of Laiians. "There are thousands of us!"

"Thousands of people that would be butchered without hesitation or remorse should that faction of my people have the opportunity. We are here to protect you, but…" Valatch spread his hands helplessly. "We must have your unceasing co-operation or we will fail – and you will die."

The doubting voice was silent, and Valatch continued relentlessly.

"Make no error in your thinking, gentlemen of Laii. King Geoffroi and my forces and I have taken a horrible risk by offering you our protection. We now suffer the certainty of dying along with you all should we be overcome – as we surely will be if we are not united against our common foe. Understand us clearly when we say that we do not intend to die here – and that one way or another there *will* be unity on this side of the Rimwall by the time our enemies' forces arrive. This is a time of great danger for us all, and while I intend to save you all, I will not endanger my people to protect you should you not fall in line immediately."

Will cleared his throat. "May we have a few minutes to talk things over in private?"

Valatch looked at Geoffroi, who nodded curtly and waved them out.

"I'm surprised that Will was their spokesman. Do you think they're going to agree?"

Valatch merely shrugged in reply and sank slowly into a chair. The two men waited in silence for the envoys' return. As the minutes passed, Geoffroi found himself growing increasingly nervous, and checked repeatedly to ensure that his warstaff was primed, and his purloined orb still nestled safely under his arm. Valatch, by contrast, seemed to sink into utter immobility. The ancient mage's only concession to the possibility of disaster was to summon a squad of guardsmen and a pair of armed magi.

Lonico

Eventually the valley men returned to the tent. They looked nervous, Geoffroi thought, and displeased by the presence of the guards and magi. They stood, silent, shifting back and forth on booted feet. Geoffroi's nose wrinkled at the earthy scent of them.

Valatch crooked an eyebrow at them, and Will stepped forward – and completely ignored the King, his brother.

"Mage Valatch, we've talked over your offer."

"And?" Valatch had risen from his chair and was looking down his vulpine nose at the men before him.

"And, we will eagerly accept your protection and co-operate with you however we can…"

Valatch's head twisted sideways, a hawk examining prey.

"I sense that you are about to say the word 'but' to me."

"Yes," murmured Will. "I am. We have talked over the situation regarding Geoff, here, and we cannot – *will* not – accept a King. Ever. Grant us this concession and we will be allies. Choose not to, and we will all die together."

Geoffroi was stunned by his brother's audacity. Stunned, and a bit amused. He sank back in his chair and laughed at the effrontery of this peasant. The idea that Valatch would – *could* – remove Geoffroi from his rightful place was unthinkable. It simply wouldn't happen – not only was Geoffroi indispensable to the work of the magi, but he was the favoured apprentice of Valatch himself. He only hoped that his mentor would decide to spare at least a few of these impudent wretches – the Valley wouldn't respond well to wanton slaughter, and if he was to reign effectively he'd need to have the…

"Done," said Valatch.

What?

"What?"

"Thank you, mage Valatch. See you later, Geoff." Will smirked at his brother, the former King.

"My guard-captains will accompany you and discuss the valley's defenses," continued Valatch. "I suggest that haste may be in order. Sush and Samaranth will not be delayed for long."

Will nodded, and the Laiians trickled out of the tent. A mage and a guardsman detached themselves from the knot of armed men in the corner and followed. There was a pause, and Valatch turned to Geoff.

Geoff could hardly see the old man through the tears of rage and humiliation that were stinging his eyes. Betrayed. Again. It would almost have been funny, if it had happened to someone else. How could people be so duplicitous? Valatch was looking at him coldly.

"I am sorry, young Geoff. Sometimes it is necessary to present people with a truly awful choice in order to force them to accept a merely bad one. From what you told me of your people, your Kingship was never a real possibility, but they needed to feel like they had wrung a major concession from me in order to secure their co-operation." The ancient mage shrugged.

Geoff sputtered. "You played me for a fool!"

"Don't be melodramatic, boy," snapped Valatch. "If you had known your part, you never would have been so odious – and you certainly never would have killed the Doctor. No, things went as they needed to. If my magi and I are to survive this, sacrifices will have to be made."

"What?"

"Samaranth and Sush – an unholy alliance brought about because of their own cowardice. Samaranth wanted to scour this Valley to the bare stone – to eradicate everyone in it forever. Sush wanted to establish a trading relationship with your people, if you can believe it. As if you were our equals, of all things! Both of them were content to talk it over endlessly, to play our standard game of consensus-building and compromise. Only I saw that something needed to be done immediately – and for that they united against me."

Geoff was shocked by the old man's rage. Flecks of spittle had appeared on the desiccated lips.

"What," he asked, "did you decide to do?"

"Why, it's simple. Your people are the bogeymen of Lonico. Children grow up terrified that you'll come screaming out of the mountains and steal their souls. The magi were given primacy, as a class, specifically to protect the city from the Monsters of the Valley of Laii. If we destroyed you, or – even more ludicrously – started treating you as potential allies, we'd remove the Great Enemy from the hearts of the people. We'd lose control. It was happening already, the old stories losing power with every year that you didn't appear."

Valatch paused for breath, and Geoff saw the old man's fingers ripple along the warstaff clutched in his hands.

"The city needs an enemy, Geoff, and you – your people – are it. I intend to arm the valley, and to set it against my home. When your people come down from your mountains, howling for Lonican blood, and are slaughtered by the magi, it will strengthen our hold on the city beyond the point that it can ever be broken. Sush and Samaranth are… complications. Nothing more. They will come around to my way of thinking, or I will kill them, or they will kill me. In any event, your people – the Laiians of myth – are forewarned and will fight for their lives. You, Geoff, were potentially useful – but you have served your purpose. It is time, I'm afraid, for you to leave us – permanently."

Valatch gestured and the magi in the corner raised their warstaves, swinging them toward Geoff. The you Laiian, however, his mind racing and diving and skittering with rage and shock, somehow moved faster. His hand dipped into the pocket near his chest, snagged the orb, and flipped it at the magi. He – and they – were unprepared for the ferocity of the resulting explosion. As Geoff flew backwards through the blackened and shredded tent wall, he had time to register that some of the magi had been reduced to pulp by the force of the orb. Then he was on his back, staring up at the sunny sky. Magi and guardsmen hurried toward him.

"As… Assassin," he wheezed. "In the tent."

The men and women scurried into the tent, warstaves at the ready, and Geoff clambered to his feet. The world still seemed to be shaking with every step, and he couldn't really hear anything, but he retained the presence of mind to stagger into the woods, where years of training took over from his battered consciousness. Like a shadow – albeit a tattered and scorched shadow, reeking of magic and blood – he flitted through the forest and was soon lost from sight among the trees.

32

"We would need more manpower, Sush – and a great deal of equipment. And time."

"Undoubtedly so, but we don't have much choice, do we? We can't breach these fortifications without unacceptable losses from our ranks, and we can't just sit here forever."

Yachem saw Samaranth shrug his frail shoulders. He and Sush were standing a little apart from the fortified camp. Excavations and earthworks now lined both sides of the bottomless – but now bridged – gorge that separated the mountain valley called Laii from the rest of the world. On this side, Sush and Samaranth's forces crouched behind hastily built breastworks. On the other, Valatch's magi took their ease in the repaired and improved fortress of Bastion. Brother glared at sister across the abyss. There was little sound but the ever-present wind, which seemed to be colder every day. The peace had a weak quality and Yachem knew that it was only a matter of time before someone did something foolish. Then, the *crump* of orbs breaking open on the rocky ground would begin, and people would start to die.

"The scouts," continued Sush, "have found the southern route into the valley. The pass through Aerie Peak is smaller and steeper, and would need to be improved somewhat, but it doesn't appear to be defended. We could have a force through there and at Valatch's back before he knew we were coming."

Samaranth straightened his hunched spine a touch, and a dry chuckle reached Yachem's ears. "I *do* like the sound of that. Very well, Sush. I will head down the mountain, meet the remainder of our forces, and send a strike group into Laii from the south. Have some of your scouts prepared to show me the way."

Lonico

Sush nodded, and beckoned Yachem toward the pair.

"Servant Yachem: Three scouts to attend mage Samaranth at the double, and supplies for a journey to be made ready."

"Yes, mage Sush." Yachem turned and began to run into the heart of camp. He was, consequently, unable to hear Samaranth's final words to Sush.

Yachem bounded into camp and rattled off Sush's orders to the appropriate people. It was odd, he thought as he caught his breath, how little things changed. After all he'd seen – after all he'd been through – he still leapt sideways at a mage's merest word. He slumped against a barrel of something that smelled like it was too long out of the sea. Eventually all of this would be done and he could, finally, go home and sort out the remainder of his life. Hopefully he'd be allowed to go work in one of the little boats that harvested guano from the islands off the coast, and he'd never have to see – let alone speak to – another mage in his life.

Yachem was granted six or seven minutes of blissful solitude before he was once again pulled into the magi's world. The runner wore no expression as she trotted up to him.

"Servant Yachem?" Her voice was soft and fluid with the sing song accent of the farmers west of the city. Yachem supposed that she was fairly pretty in a muscular farm-girl way, and was so shocked and appalled at his betrayal of Taia that he barely mumbled a curt reply.

"Yes."

"Orders from mage Samaranth, servant." Yachem noticed that she had chosen the formal mode of address rather than the more usual familiar. Had he insulted her somehow? "You are to return to the city in his cadre for reassignment. Report to his tent ready to travel before first light tomorrow."

Home. His deliverance would come sooner than hoped. He wouldn't have to watch Geoff and Daniel's families slaughtered, or see their lands burned. "Thank you, guard…?"

The runner didn't take the opportunity to share her name. She merely nodded once and slipped back into the swirl of guards, servants, and magi. Yachem watched her go, and then stood. He had a lot to do before first light, and he was going to need some sleep – at some point. He stepped into the flow of humanity and allowed it to carry him to his tent.

A little way off, a guardsman took his ease on top of a pile of sacks. He was a large man, by the standards of his city, and watched the world through eyes that appeared to belong to a simple, brutish, and violent man. Ganarae was, in point of fact, none of those things, although he was a convincing enough mimic to have risen to (and stalled at) the rank of guard-sergeant. It was a position that called for simplicity, directness, and brutality. Ganarae pulled it off with, he thought, a certain verve. It was not, however, his primary function.

A sing song voice called from the shadow of a nearby tent. "He's wrapped up in *them*, Ganarae. Couldn't even be bothered to be polite to a mere servant anymore. Looked right through me."

"Now, Orchel, don't be in such a hurry to judge. Servant Yachem has been through an awful lot in the last few months – between his adventure over-mountain and his wife's murder – so he's bound..."

"His wife's murder? Who killed her?"

"Depending on who you believe, Yachem himself, some madman from Laii or somewhere, or a mage proving a point. Anyway, as I was saying, he's bound to be a bit out of sorts."

"I'd say so."

"As would I. Orchel, I believe that servant Yachem might be amenable to our ideas and, moreover, may be extraordinarily useful to our efforts. I believe that one of us should return to the city with him and sound him out further. The other shall remain here. Preference?"

Orchel didn't answer immediately. After a long pause, she sighed.

"As much as I'd like to go home, as a guardsman you're in danger here. We can't afford to lose you to some pointless power struggle between the magi. You go."

Ganarae nodded slowly.

"I'll arrange to have myself named to Samaranth's bodyguard. I'll be in touch as soon as I can, Orchel. Be careful up here."

Orchel didn't answer, and when Ganarae turned his head to look at her she had already gone.

Lonico

33

Yachem couldn't help but feel that the thuggish guard-sergeant was watching him. The hulking man had tiny little shark-like eyes, which were at once emotionless and threatening. Most worryingly, occasionally when Yachem glanced toward the thug, he saw those black eyes flick away from his face. It was unsettling, to say the least, but there was nothing to be done about it. The man had obviously been set to watch him by the magi, and to even voice a question about the situation was to invite swift punishment. Yachem stole another glance at the broad-shouldered man, who turned abruptly and made a show of regarding a distant tree.

Yachem sighed. The small party was crawling down the mountainside, nearly at the forest. He sincerely hoped that this would be the last time he ever had to cross through that forsaken place. Quite apart from its oppressive nature, with its grasping branches and dark copses, the forest was too full of unhappy thoughts for Yachem. Between Priest, and Daniel, and of course Guise – the entire place was just unendurable.

He shook his head and swallowed another sigh. Looking up, he saw the expressionless eyes of the Sergeant on him – again – and this time it could not pass without comment.

"What do you want?" The question escaped Yachem's throat in a ragged, querulous yelp. Not the most dignified demand, perhaps, but it was all he could manage. The Sergeant had the good grace to shrug and look away. This time, his gaze did not return to Yachem.

The afternoon sun tipped below the jagged horizon and daylight was lifted from the land before the small column of men halted for the night.

For two more days they woke and walked and slept, and soon they found themselves approaching the ghost town of Westford.

Immediately, Yachem was reminded of the first time he had been through the town – the feeling of eyes in the forest, and the prickling on the back of the neck as the travelers were sized up. There was the same lack of birdsong in the trees now, the same too-still silence, and Yachem was sure that the little cadre was not alone in the woods. He began to see faces in every shadow, and to imagine that every branch was a raised bow. As they made camp in the ruined town that evening, Yachem couldn't understand why there had been no attack. The presence of Samaranth and the five magi he'd brought as protection – not to mention the dozen guardsmen – was a deterrent, to be sure, but surely not enough of one.

Yachem slept poorly that night, huddled in the crook of a broken-down statue's marble arm, and woke with a start every time the patrolling guardsmen scuffed their feet on the cobbles of the dead city.

The next morning broke clear and cold, and the ferns crunched under their boots as the little procession hurried south. Yachem's fears of yesterday seemed remote as summer. Much of the servant's attention was devoted to keeping the frail Samaranth firmly atop his horse. The old man tired quickly in the cold, and the group's progress was slow.

They had just cleared the ruins of Westford when the bushes on either side of the path shuddered and disgorged a flight of arrows and a mass of green-clad men. Four servants and a mage were on the ground screaming before Yachem even turned his head to focus on the hollering attackers. Silvery swords flashed in outstretched hands as the gap between the tiny caravan and the raiders narrowed.

Then, time shuddered to a near halt. There, right in the middle of the snarling horde, a small man grinned a gap-toothed grin at Yachem as he charged forward. Guise. A voice floated over Yachem's shoulder, sliding through the tiny gaps of quiet in the tumult – somehow clearly audible through the noise.

"Fan pattern," it said. "Now."

And then Yachem was thrown face first onto the ground when someone's boot struck him between the shoulder blades, and he didn't see what happened next. He heard a sound like branches snapping again and again and again and eventually he just covered his ears and tried not to breathe in the magic, and tried not to imagine what was happening to Guise's people. The sound went on for a while – maybe a moment, maybe an hour – and then Yachem was grabbed by the neck and hauled to his feet. Far too dazed to resist or even question, he was deep among the boles of the uncaring trees before he realized that things were still getting worse. The stench of festering meat surrounded him, and he turned his head. Guise's rotten mouth grinned at him from a distance of a few inches.

"I'm gonna kill yer now, servant."

Yachem's fear left him, all of a sudden, as the patent unfairness of the situation overwhelmed all of his other concerns. *He'd* been dragged up and down the world again and again at the whim of the magi. *He'd* lost friends left and right. *He* had been separated from his wife far, far too early. And now this thug was threatening him again? Not today.

Yachem's fist snaked out and clipped Guise – hard – on the point of his chin. The small man's head snapped back and he staggered a few heavy steps, and then Yachem was on him. His fists hammered into the little monster over and over, face and knuckles bruising and breaking each other. Yachem didn't know when Guise stopped fighting back, and he wouldn't have cared. Eventually the rage that had spurred him on was spent, and he stepped away from the still form of his tormentor.

Everything was quiet. Yachem turned in place, trying to figure out how to return to the path, and the survivors of this latest disaster.

A sound caught his ear from behind him, and Yachem turned again.

"Fer that, I'm gonna kill yer *slow*."

Guise stood, unsteady but undeniably upright. A long knife glinted in a hand extended toward Yachem. For a moment, all Yachem could do was gape at the sheer relentlessness of this man, and at the knowledge that Guise would follow him for the rest of his days. What was the point of fighting any more? It wasn't like Yachem had anything to live for, beyond catering to the whims of people who couldn't care less if he lived or died. He sighed and slumped and that hand, holding that knife, slid closer to his throat. Yachem closed his eyes and waited. All at once, there was a yelp, a thump, and a spray of warmth on his face. He opened his eyes to see Guise staring down at the abbreviated stump of his arm. Yachem's eyes tracked left to alight upon the expedition's burly sergeant, standing with a bloodied sword in his hand.

"This man killed my wife," stammered the servant.

"So I'd heard," replied the sergeant. "And all things considered, I thought you might like to do the honours."

The sergeant reversed the blade and extended it, hilt first, to Yachem. The servant took the sword from the guard's hand.

"Yes," he said, and shoved the blade gracelessly into Guise's chest. The weapon was keen, and slid home with little resistance. Guise's mouth filled with blood, and his eyes drained of the hatefulness that had animated them. He collapsed to the ground, and suddenly he was just a small dead man – no longer the specter who had haunted Yachem for so many days and weeks and months.

Yachem handed the sword back to his savior. "Here you are, guardsman-sergeant. I suppose we had best be getting back to the magi so I can thank them for sending you after me."

The sergeant snorted derisively as they began to walk through the trees. "Thank *them*? Samaranth told me not to bother coming after you at all. I told him I'd catch up by noon, one way or the other. You don't owe *them* any thanks at all."

Yachem nodded slowly. "I'm sorry, guardsman-sergeant. I owe my thanks to you."

"Pfft. You don't owe me anything either. It's what people do for each other when they're in trouble. Or at least, they *should*. It's just the damn magi who mess things up."

Yachem shrugged noncommittally. Carefully. Was this man really being so openly hostile to the magi? Every part of Yachem's mind screamed the word "trap" over and over.

The sergeant regarded him for a moment as they walked.

"My name's Ganarae," he said, "and I think we have a lot to talk about."

Lonico

34

Geoff crept through the low-lying shrubs running along the stream's edge. He was taking care not to disturb any of the loose stones of the bank as he moved – the resulting grind and crash would be loud and distinctive should anyone be listening. It had been three days since Valatch's betrayal at the clearing, and they had not been good ones for Geoff. Sleeping wedged between the branches of trees, wading through streams, avoiding everyone – city man *or* Laiian – who wandered by... it had taken Geoff a day and a half to steal himself a good solid set of valley clothes to replace the tattered and useless frippery of the magi. Even now, creeping toward the isolated farm that Geoff hoped would supply his dinner, he was conscious of that supreme dishonesty – of the absolute callousness of these men and women who would use any person in any way to achieve their inscrutable ends. He still felt the phantom brush of smooth silk on his neck and wrists, and prayed that one day soon he would not.

He inched closer to the farm's little vegetable patch – the turnips would be ripest, he thought, and the farmer would be unlikely to miss them. Unlikely to miss them too soon, at least. Geoff's need was greater, anyway. Geoff looked up at the sun, slipping quickly toward the western Rimwall. Dusk would be on the valley in minutes, he reckoned, and protective night would soon follow. Geoff settled in to wait for his opportunity.

He was soon drowsing, and in his troubled dreams it seemed to Geoff that the screech of crickets and the babble of the river had become the screeches of terrified children and the babble of voices raised in anger. He came awake, all at once, but for long minutes wasn't sure if the sounds he was hearing were real or the creations of his mind. Cautiously he raised his head above the bushes. Bright-burning lamps spangled the field in front of the farmhouse, illuminating many shadowed forms milling about. A series of shouts, their meaning incomprehensible in the distance, were followed by a sudden rush of movement and a scream, high with terror and pain. Everything went very still, and far too quiet. There was a stirring in the crowd, and three lamps arced up and over, and a great rose of flame bloomed on the roof of the farmhouse.

Two magi and their cadre of guardsmen were abruptly illuminated. One of the magi, a large man whose robe strained against rolls of fat, shoved a tiny figure into the rapidly burning house and slammed the door. He giggled, the high-pitched sound clear even over the distance and the growing roar of the fire. Geoff heard that giggle, and immediately knew who the large mage was. Valatch had told Geoff that this mage, Oktel by name, had displayed an unwholesome joy in the act of torment. Geoff had been warned to steer clear, and had seen proof of Valatch's claim firsthand after the attack in the forest. That same giggle had rung out as Oktel had repeatedly probed the oozing wound of a fallen guardsman with his warstaff. The prone Lonican had screamed, and Oktel's laugh had gone on and on and on.

Geoff decided in that instant that he had never really liked Oktel, and as the small group of city folk turned from the fire, Geoff followed at a distance. The magi walked slowly down the path into the woods, the guardsmen trailing behind, burdened with pilfered supplies. The group made glacial progress through the early evening, and then came to a stop at a widening in the path. Geoff stepped behind a tree and watched as the guardsmen kicked off their boots and relaxed. Soon, only Oktel and the other mage – a woman with whom Geoff had never so much as spoken – were awake.

"We can't rest long, Oktel. Valatch wants all of the patrols back by first light."

"Mmm."

"So when should we move out, do you think?"

"I don't know. Give the guards another ten minutes and carry on."

The other mage paused from digging the pebbles out of her boot soles with a knife. "What do you mean by that?"

Oktel snorted. "I mean carry on, woman. I'm going back to that farm. I don't think we quite finished up, there."

Lonico

"Alone? Are you insane? This is not the city, Oktel. We aren't undisputed lords and masters here yet."

"Bah. This valley is broken, and Sush's people are still days away from trying anything. I'll be fine, and I don't want to leave anything… unfinished." The giggle erupted from his throat once again and he grinned at the woman, who threw her hands up in disgust.

"Do what you want, then. I'll try to cover for you if Valatch asks any questions."

"Thank you, my dear. I expected nothing less from you. I'll be back at camp by mid-morning."

Oktel laughed again, loudly enough to wake the few guards whose sleep was still unfeigned, and turned back up the path. He passed the tree behind which Geoff was hiding at a distance of no more than ten feet, and then faded into the dark.

Geoff hesitated for a moment, and then slipped through the trees after him. It was only after Oktel's blood was drenching his hands – and the hefty stick he'd used to kill him – that Geoff paused to wonder whether he could have helped the farmer and his family any earlier.

He shrugged in the darkness and continued to strip Oktel's corpse of everything useful. The family probably couldn't be helped, and the chance to arm himself – and get some clean clothes – was too good to pass up.

By the time he hurried up the path toward the burned-out farmhouse, his newfound burdens pressing into the flesh and bones of his back, the silver of the coming dawn was already staining the night. He came to a halt as he crested a rise and the farm came into view, well aware that he was far too late. The fire had cooled, and only a few scattered embers glared sullenly up into the waning night. The farmer and his family were dead, without question. Geoff's mind shuddered back self-protectively from a closer inspection of their twisted and scorched bodies. He gazed at the confusion and terror that had once been a home and, for the first time, wondered how much of it had been his fault. He turned in place and looked out over the valley, revealing itself in the growing light. This house, on its little hill, had commanded an excellent view.

He tried not to imagine a father standing in this very spot, telling his young son of the valley that would be his home. The sun slowly filled the valley with pale autumn light – it would turn cold in days, from the looks of things – and as the light grew, Geoff saw the smoke. It was rising, not in the well-ordered grey strands of cooking-fires, but in the gouting black billows of many uncontrolled burns, and it was rising from sources all around the valley. The magi were tightening their grip – snuffing out resistance even as they kindled these fires. Geoff realized that the burnings were also part of Valatch's plan. Only by infuriating the Laiians could he goad them to action against the city. If he hadn't been so blind, so willing to believe that he needed to avenge some imaginary slight against him, his valley wouldn't be burning.

Geoff shook his head slowly. How was he going to fix this? Daniel would know what to do. The old 'hand had always known what to do. He wished that Valatch hadn't goaded Geoff into killing the fool. What would Daniel do in this situation? Simple: He'd find Geoff's family and make sure they were alright, and then he'd do whatever was necessary to dislodge the parasites that had infected their home. Geoff needed to find Will. The thought bloomed in his head simultaneously with coruscating sparks of light and pain, and he flew forward into darkness.

35

Geoff woke up naked, and tied to a rugged old pine tree. He struggled, groggy and confused, against his ropes for a little while, and succeeded only in scraping his back and wrists until they bled. He stopped and cast his eyes around. He was still in the valley, definitely. The smell, the texture of the air, the coolness in the air, there was no doubt. Trees grew thickly all about, twisting around each other as they climbed slowly toward the light. There was the smell of a distant wood fire, and a few birds chirped in the branches.

Probably somewhere in the southern forest, he thought, near the old Aerie Peak. It was the only place in the valley where loose firewood was this plentiful, especially with winter coming on in a few months. Geoff's pack rested against the trunk of a tree a few dozen paces away, and the three charged warstaves he'd liberated from Oktel lay on the ground beside it. *Might as well be sitting at the bottom of the river, for all the good they're doing me right now.* He tried his bonds again, failed once more to loosen them, and subsided.

Despite his apparent solitude, Geoff was fairly sure that he wasn't alone. There weren't quite enough birds singing, he decided after a while, especially in the area directly ahead of him. He peered through the branches, attempting to resolve a shape or figure. All he achieved was a massive and insistent headache. Someone had hit him on the head, and had done it *hard*. He sighed and waited, watching the shadows swing through midday and into the afternoon. The bugs found him quickly and, knowing a good thing when they saw one, quickly went to work. Before long, he was bleeding from a hundred tiny wounds to his belly, arms, and scalp.

A face appeared and vanished among the trees. Soon the birds went entirely silent and a group of valley men appeared, Will at its head.

Geoff smiled, and only then realized how dehydrated he was. His lips cracked and split with the effort. Will sighed and strode forward, a waterskin appearing in his hand. A slow trickle of water passed Geoff's lips.

"Thank you, Will," he croaked. "Thank you."

"You're welcome, Geoffroi," replied Will.

Geoff cringed a little. "Just Geoff is fine, thanks."

Will glared at his brother. "What am I supposed to do with you? If I turn you over to *them*," he gestured irritably to the northeast, "they'll kill you."

He stabbed a thumb over his shoulder at the small group of men behind him. "If I turn you over to them, *they'll* probably kill you too.

I'm tempted to kill you myself for what you did to that family last night."

Geoff sputtered for a moment, trying to force a hundred words out of his mouth at once. He finally settled on one.

"No! You've got everything backwards. I didn't burn down the house or hurt those people. I was there, yes. To steal some food! Then these magi came and killed the family and I followed them and I killed one – Oktel – and then I went back to see if there was anything I could do to help!"

Will had taken a step back, apparently startled by his brother's sudden vehemence, and Geoff pressed on. His panic was subsiding, now, and words no longer erupted from his mouth a dozen at a time.

"They turned on me. I know I was wrong to lead them here but they killed Daniel," the lie was a convenient one and Geoff was sure that even he would come to believe it eventually, "and they told me that I had to do what they said."

Geoff could see that he was losing them. Nobody here really cared for excuses. Nobody in the valley ever really did. It was the sort of place where, if you wronged someone, you just fixed the problem and everything was quickly forgotten. Life was too hard to worry about grudges – or to waste energy trying to explain. He cast his eyes wildly around the glade. His gaze fell upon his pack, forlorn beside the tree.

Suddenly he remembered Daniel's kindly face – remembered the old 'hand telling Geoff of the times that he'd swum across the mouth of the swirling, sucking Hole in the river. When he'd taken his life up into his hands and put it all into one endeavor that would lead either to glory or to the cool darkness beneath the mountains. Something clicked in Geoff's mind.

He took a deep breath and swam the Hole.

"I've stolen some of their magic." He nodded at the pack and the warstaves near it. "I can teach you to use it – anyone can learn. I can teach you to fight them. We can kick them out of our valley and take back our homes. If you let me free, I will make good the wrong I have done."

Lonico

A sudden stir ran through the men gathered around him, and Geoff knew that he teetered on the very edge of life and death. If these people – if *his* people – were even marginally loyal to the Magi, then everything was over. He clamped his eyes onto Will's, straining to discern a hint of what he was thinking. Then, very slowly and deliberately, Will winked at Geoff.

"Now, Smithson," he called, and there was a sudden movement at the back of the crowd. A man collapsed in an untidy heap.

"Michael has been pushing us to co-operate with them right from the beginning," Will said. "We couldn't take the risk. We'll keep an eye on him and hopefully when this is all over, he'll forgive us. He's going to be okay, right Jacob? You didn't hit him too hard?"

Jacob Smithson, already nearly as large as his father, grinned from the back of the crowd and brandished a length of wood in his hand.

"No harder than I hit Geoff."

Will smiled and cut through the ropes that bound Geoff to the tree. As the last coil fell away, he leaned in close to his brother.

"There will be no more betrayals from you," he murmured. It was not a question, but Geoff answered anyway.

"There will be no more betrayals, Will."

Will smiled and clapped Geoff on the shoulder.

"Let's get you some clothes, then. You're embarrassing yourself."

36

Yachem was dismissed almost immediately upon the little group's arrival in the city. His spirits had been rising consistently for several hours as the splendour of his home grew ever closer. Now that he was inside Lonico, with the sounds and sights and stenches of his people surrounding him again, he didn't know how he had ever left.

There is a peculiar way, he thought, that your vision is restricted in this city. Between the anarchic twisting of the streets themselves, the surging crowds, and the constant haze of wood and coal smoke blueing the air, you could never really see what was coming until it was right on top of you.

Yachem was so caught up in the experience of being home, of walking the same streets that he'd walked for his entire life, that he almost forgot about Taia. Almost. For a moment. Then he walked past a servant in a dress that Taia might have made and his buoyancy left him. He turned to see Samaranth watching him with rheumy, calculating little eyes. The old mage's voice cut effortlessly through the noise of the crowd.

"You will take your ease today, servant, and then tomorrow you will report to the Tower for reassignment. You are literate, correct?"

Yachem nodded dumbly, and Samaranth smiled – like the unsheathing of a rusty knife.

"Excellent. Something in the Bureaucracy, then. Your reward for such faithful service." The mage turned away before Yachem could respond.

Yachem stood alone for a moment, and then hurried off to meet Ganarae. He thought that the big guard-sergeant would be pleased with this development.

A few minutes later he hurried into a low building near the docklands. Men and women – servants all – sat at rough wood tables, tankards close to hand. Servingmen threaded through the noisy crowd, distributing drinks and collecting dull metal *dok* in exchange. To all appearances, then, it was a normal tavern. Appearances, in this case, were deceiving. Ganarae had told him all about *The Mage's Staff and Orbs* on the long trip back to Lonico. Over several days of furtive conversation, Ganarae had worn away at Yachem's suspicions and had finally convinced the servant that he was being genuine. He had also convinced the servant that he was not alone. Others in the city yearned for freedom from the hegemony of the magi.

Yachem was conscious of eyes on him, of slightly shifted postures and choked-off conversations as he walked across the room. At a small table in the back, he saw Ganarae speaking quietly with a tanned and rugged sailor. Yachem waited out of earshot, but Ganarae waved him into a chair.

"We don't stand on formality here, Yachem, and you're always welcome at my table. This won't take a minute." The Sergeant turned his attention back to the sailor and resumed speaking. Yachem could feel the mood in the room shift again — obviously Ganarae's invitation to sit was something of import to this group — and he took the opportunity to order a drink. It arrived speedily, and before Yachem could dig out from his pockets the *doh* it cost, Ganarae flipped a coin to the serving-man and waved him away.

Yachem looked up, and was surprised to see that the sailor had disappeared into the crowd. Ganarae was looking at him, amusement in his eyes.

"I hear," the soldier said, "that you have some news for me."

Yachem started in surprise. "How did you hear about *that*?"

"We have our sources." Ganarae waggled his eyebrows theatrically. "Actually, we simply make it a point to listen — whenever we can — to everything the magi have to say. There are enough of us that we can usually follow the important ones, at least when they're out in the city. Congratulations on your reassignment."

"Thank you, Ganarae. I was hoping that it might be useful for us to have someone inside the Bureaucracy. If we're ever going to bring them —"

Ganarae held up a hand to interrupt Yachem's speech.

"There are some things we never speak of in the city, my friend, no matter the situation. Were the merest hint that we feel as we do to reach the ears of the magi, not one of us would survive the night. We work towards that end, of course, but the time is not yet right for overt action. We plan, we gather our strength, and we wait. Clear?"

Yachem nodded, deeply chastened. Ganarae grinned at him.

"To answer your question though, Yachem, yes. You're tremendously valuable to us. Firstly, the simple fact that you're sympathetic to our aims makes you more valuable than gold. Your new position gives us another thread of information to tug on. Your involvement in this insane crusade against the Laiians gives us insight into that situation that we would otherwise lack. You can read and write, which is a skill that not more than four or five of us possess. Oh, you're valuable to us, Yachem. I'd go so far as to say that finding you is something of a coup."

Yachem found that he was actually blushing. Praise was rare enough in a servant's life that it had a profound effect on them.

The two men talked late into the night, occasionally joined by other members of Yachem's new fraternity. Men and women with fanciful assumed names like Staffsplitter or The Hook – all of whom referred to Yachem as Brains. Ganarae's was the only real name anyone seemed to know.

The conversations darted from topic to topic like schooling fish. All the while, Yachem felt a sense of belonging and acceptance grow in his belly. As they all danced carefully around their shared hatred of the magi, and their common goal, Yachem began to believe that they might actually be able to change things in the city. Freedom was a new concept to Yachem, and a difficult one, but he was a keen student.

The sun was resting on the ocean like a ball as Yachem walked across the low servants bridge that connected the city of Lonico to the Island of the Magi. To his groggy eyes, the towers silhouetted against the sun looked like some undersea monster's ragged talons, reaching up to claw at the sky. He hurried along the bridge and nearly ran toward the tower of the Council. It would not do to be late on his first day. He paused for a moment to collect himself when he reached the massive engraved doors of the tower, and smoothed his hair back from his forehead.

The guards posted outside the tower looked him up and down briefly, and one of them waved him in. Opening the small sally-port, he stepped through. At this hour, the Bureau was mostly quiet. Only a few servants scratched away at their tables. Yachem thrilled to know that he would soon be among them.

A Bureaucrat glanced at him from her desk near the door.

"Servant Yachem?"

Yachem nodded.

"Mage Samaranth is waiting for you." The woman gestured to the elevating-platform, and Yachem stepped onto it. Vast gears clanked, and the platform lurched into movement – down. Sudden panic gripped Yachem. Samaranth's office was at the pinnacle of the tower. There was nothing *down*, except… Yachem couldn't finish the thought.

The platform continued its inexorable descent into the bowels of the island, and Yachem's fears grew with every moment. Suddenly the platform slowed and ground to a halt. No opening pierced the wall. No exit. Finally, whoever was running this contraption had realized their mistake and would soon get him going in the right direction. Relief flooded through Yachem, welcome as a fire in winter, as he waited for the platform to heave itself skyward.

A small cough echoed from behind him, and Yachem spun on his heel. Samaranth and two other magi stood in an otherwise empty and featureless hallway. A single low door squatted behind them.

"I trust that you had an informative evening," croaked Samaranth with an evil smile. "Take him."

The two magi at Samaranth's shoulder flowed smoothly toward Yachem, who backed away as far as he could. Finding no place of refuge on the platform, the servant charged. He bowled one of the two magi to the ground and dealt the other a blow that sent him staggering into a wall.

Yachem spun and gathered his legs to launch himself at Samaranth. In the tiny instant before he could spring, the mage's hand whipped forward like lightning. *Something* darted from Samaranth's fingertips and burst at Yachem's feet. An eruption of light and sound and choking smoke shocked the servant into momentary stillness and before he could recover he felt the butt of a warstaff slam into his stomach. He collapsed.

Ancient Samaranth hobbled to Yachem, drew back a booted foot, and kicked him in the ribs. Yachem felt something crack, and he curled into a tight ball. Samaranth's henchmen, finally recovered from Yachem's sudden attack, strode forward and yanked him to his feet. His arms and legs were quickly shackled.

Samaranth glared at Yachem's captors.

"Take everything he knows. Spare no measures. Kill him when you have it all. Exterminate this *Resistance*. Report the results to me immediately. Know that your continued existence relies upon your success."

The two magi glanced at each other, bowed deeply to Samaranth, and dragged Yachem toward the low door at the end of the hallway.

Within minutes, screams echoed throughout the tower. The Bureaucrats worked diligently and fast that day.

37

Jacob Smithson dragged the last guardsman, finally quiet and still, into the shallow gully and covered him over with fallen leaves. The boy really was inhumanly strong and seemed, thought Geoff, to be fairly intelligent as well. He had certainly seemed to grasp the theory behind the warstaves quickly enough, and he claimed that there was some sort of mechanical basis to the magi's magic. Geoff hadn't understood a word of Jacob's explanation of the forces involved, but believed him nonetheless. He smiled to himself for a moment when he realized that he'd thought of Smithson as a boy – he was six months Geoff's senior.

Jacob turned toward the small rise where Geoff and Will were standing and flashed a white grin. Will chuckled quietly. This ambush had gone smoothly, unlike the last one. This time, only pale city men writhed on the ground after the smoke cleared. This time there were no sudden tears as the pellets ejected by the warstaves made every wound, no matter how apparently minor, a fatal one. This time a course of arrows had scoured the path from the deep cover of the surrounding woods, and had immediately been followed by a discharge of the strange energies stored in the warstaves. This time, the two magi strutting along the path as if they had walked it their whole lives had been cut down before they could un-sling their weapons, and their guards had survived little longer.

More proof that this place was not safe for the city-born. Six more dead guardsmen. Two more dead magi. Valatch must have fewer than thirty of them, now. He'd need to pull back their mage-led patrols, or risk being fatally weakened when the great push came from Sush's forces. Geoff knew that he'd have to stop killing magi at some point. Sush and Samaranth couldn't be allowed to reach the valley – at least not without Valatch seriously bloodying their noses first. Playing the two sides off against each other was an impossibly delicate task, but the only way to survive.

He glanced at Will and his brother looked back, a satisfied smile on his face. Geoff had been startled to discover that Will took to fighting like a bird took to the air. At first there had been a great deal of commotion and noise, but now every motion seemed smooth, practiced, and natural. The men followed him as if he'd been bred to lead. Of course, Will had always been awesomely, frustratingly competent – but Geoff had believed warfare might be the exception. No such luck. Surprisingly, the old feelings of jealousy were completely absent in Geoff.

Will held up four calloused fingers. Four more warstaves for the nascent army. That made a total of sixteen – as well as five of the red orbs. Not enough magic, of course, for Geoff to engage Valatch's people in a pitched battle. Maybe, however, enough for them to turn the course of a battle between Valatch and Samaranth.

A sibilant whisper slipped between the trees to Geoff's ears, and his head snapped around. Micah – a young 'hand from a farm near Citadel – stepped out of the forest and swept his hand downward in a wide arc. The remainder of the growing band – twenty-five men and women, now – stopped their chatter and faded into near invisibility in the underbrush. Geoff wriggled under a blackberry bush, ignoring the thorns that raked his exposed hands and neck, and trusted in stillness and the natural camouflage of his brown and green clothing to keep him hidden. What the hell could be going on now? Another patrol so soon?

The smell of leaves and earth and fallen fruit filled his nose. Moments stretched into minutes before a distant sound echoed through the trees and a flash of colour bloomed and vanished among the tangled branches. The lilting, too-formal sound of city-folk speech reached his ears, and Geoff's mind raced. They had obviously been outflanked – perhaps this last patrol had been nothing more than bait. He wouldn't put it past Valatch to spend men in such a fashion.

Geoff caught Will's eye and mimed the priming of a warstaff. Will nodded and gestured at someone out of Geoff's view. There was a slight rustling through the forest – as if a sudden breeze had arisen – while the Laiians prepared their warstaves, their bows, and their clubs. The rustling faded, and again the only sound was of Lonicans blundering through the woods. Will and Geoff aimed their warstaves toward the sound. The men would attack on their signal. Hopefully. If someone lost his nerve and shot too early… Geoff abandoned the line of thought. The consequences were too terrible to consider too closely. The noise of the approaching force grew ever louder.

When the first elements strode into view, Geoff's eyes widened. Magi and guardsmen by the score threaded through the forest – and Geoff didn't recognize a single one. Valatch had brought more men up from some hidden reserve. He watched as brightly clad men and women filed through the woods. Something in their bearing, furtive despite the noise they were making, seemed significant to Geoff. Why would Valatch's magi be trying to hide? Suddenly, it clicked into place. This was not an ambush set by Valatch, but a force set to *kill* Valatch. Geoff was certain of it. Sush must have found – or made – another route into the valley.

The procession inched by, Geoff amazed every second that not one of the hidden Laiians was discovered. Eventually the final guardsman stumbled, cursing, out of view and the forest was again quiet. As if possessing some innate magic of their own, Laiians materialized in the spaces between the trees and approached Will and Geoff. Worried faces predominated. Will held up a hand to them, and pulled Geoff aside.

"Well," said Will. "That changes things a bit. What are we going to do, Geoff? Can we even fight that… that… *that?*"

"The only thing that this changes is that we no longer have a choice in the matter, Will. Those weren't Valatch's people who just strolled past us. Those ones belong to Sush or, worse, to Samaranth. Either way, we're in real trouble now – they were headed for Market."

Will blanched, the colour seeming to drain from under his years-earned tan.

"They'll be slaughtered. The valley would never recover."

"Yes. Unless we do something."

Will nodded. "First things first, then."

He spun on his heel to face the tiny, filthy band of men and women who were suddenly the hope of everything he had ever known. Geoff saw his brother straighten as he gestured them all close, and for the first time in his life was proud to be related to a great man.

"Those people who went by are headed to Market, folks, and they aren't after a new plough-blade. If they make it there before we do, your families, your friends, and your lives are going to be ashes. There will be nothing left by the time the sun goes down, unless you all do exactly as I say."

Grips tightened on warstaves, on bows, on wavering nerves. Grown men swallowed nervously, and farm wives nodded resolutely.

"Most of us are going to go to Market. We'll try to beat the magi there, and save the people that we can save. But I need five volunteers who know how to use a warstaff. Five volunteers who – well, in all likelihood, will be a memory by the end of the day."

Feet shuffled and nerves thrilled. Everything, Geoff, imagined, had suddenly become very real for these people. No more jumping unsuspecting, outnumbered magi from the shadows, now. This would be nothing but a glorious death… or maybe a redemptive one. Geoff sighed and stepped forward.

"I'll go," he said. "The people at Market have little enough reason to follow me anywhere."

Will peered at him for a moment, and then smiled.

"Good. Anyone else?"

One by one, hands rose. Jason stepped forward, and Micah. Owyn and Aline, twins from the north side of the valley who apparently never did anything separately, rounded out the group. They all shook hands solemnly.

"I guess I get to make up for bashing your head in," grinned Smith, and Geoff smiled back.

Will glowered the pair into silence. "I need you five to take a staff each. Circle around to the east, and then start hitting that column. Sting them, slow them, draw them away from Market if you can. Buy us time to get the people away by whatever means necessary."

There was no mention of keeping safe. It probably wasn't possible. Five heads nodded. Geoff felt his throat go dry.

"As long as there's a Laii," continued Will, "people will remember this. Now get going."

Geoff would have laughed if he could have – more than anyone living, perhaps, he knew how much of their history the people of this valley had forgotten. He gestured to his men – and woman – and they hurriedly began to collect warstaves and pellets and the strange black powder that would allow them to use the magic of Lonico. Satisfied that they were well-provisioned, Geoff nodded and led his troupe into the woods at a run. As they hurried through the trees, Will's instructions to the others echoed after them.

"Split up. Get to Market. Get the people out. Meet two miles west along the river with anyone willing to fight. Run."

Geoff and his band sprinted through the trees toward the eastern Rim for a few minutes, and then turned north. As they settled into the ground-chewing trot that most Laiians could keep up all day, Geoff began to hiss instructions.

"We can't hope to outgun them. If we spread out, we'll be dead. We need to stick together, fire everything at once, and then retreat into the trees and do it again. Aim for magi, or for any guardsman who has silver stripes on his arm, like so. Stay mobile and stay quiet until we strike. Do not, under any circumstances, allow yourself to be taken alive. Got it?"

Four heads bobbed and they ran onwards. The three blue orbs that he'd kept for himself clinked softly against his chest. Hopefully they'd hold together for this run. The Laiians flitted through the trees like malevolent forest spirits, every ounce of their concentration now devoted to speed.

Nearly two miles away, Will scythed through the forest. Far and away the fittest son of a fittest son of a fittest son, Will was built for this sort of thing. He was, moreover, moving through territory that he had walked every day of his life, and supremely well-motivated to make every stride count. They had been seven miles of scrub forest and rutted fields from Market when they'd sighted the magi and their flunkies. Will made the run in forty minutes.

He skidded to a halt in the center of the town, curious and alarmed faces peering at him from all angles. With harvest coming up so soon, as well as the general terror that had gripped Laii, Market was crowded with people. Some, the battered, fearful looking ones, had left burning farms behind to come to Market and its illusory safety. Most were looking to have repairs done on equipment, or simply to enjoy a gossip before the hard work needed to be done. There was certainly enough to gossip about, enough to knock the simple life of the Laiians completely off-kilter, but the simple fact of harvest was incontrovertible. In a few days or weeks, the weather would make its turn and *everything* would have to be put aside except the simple, monotonous acts of reaping, culling, picking, and the rest. There was no option to delay or ignore the changing seasons, even for Will himself. Starvation would empty the valley more surely than any war.

Raising his fingers to his mouth, he gave a piercing whistle. The few heads that hadn't turned to follow his dash and skidding stop turned toward him now. He began to speak loudly and clearly. It didn't take long.

Geoff moved his head – slowly – around the trunk of the tree. *There they are. Finally.* Samaranth's column of invaders had been making terrible time. It had taken them nearly an hour to reach the spot Geoff had selected for the first ambush. The soldiers and their magi came crunching and clanking through the woods, meandering along the easiest route north. The path they followed had brought the force to a shallow marsh – once Geoff's favourite place to trap the ducks that arrived in the summer. He flicked his eyes to the northwest and noticed with relief that the threads of smoke rising from Market had been cut off at their bases, and had quickly begun to blur into the clouding sky. Will was doing his job. He turned his attention back to the matter at hand.

He raised his warstaff and sighted along its length. The plan was simple. Kill some magi, scatter, regroup, and repeat. He wished that he knew what Samaranth looked like. *That* would be something of a coup. He checked the position of the sun, quickly dipping behind the trees on the far side of the swamp even though the afternoon was still young. Shadowy fingers caressed the surface of the swamp's stagnant waters. Even forty paces away, Geoff could hear the rising whine of tiny biting flies. He grinned, and waited for the perfect moment.

The lead elements of the army had reached the edge of the swamp and slowly turned to move around it. The gnats and mosquitoes descended upon the Laiians in a bloodthirsty cloud, and guardsmen and magi began to slap ineffectually at their unseen tormentors. Geoff rather hoped that was an omen.

He picked out a target – a chubby, sweating mage already bleeding from a dozen fly-bites – drew a breath, and released the magic. An earsplitting crack and a purple cloud erupted from the far end of the warstaff and was echoed by his compatriots' attacks. Beside him Aline cursed and shook her staff, which had unaccountably refused to work. The sweating mage tumbled to the ground, where he was joined by two of his companions, each writhing momentarily and then falling still as the magic did its evil work. The column seemed, for a moment, to fold in upon itself in shock, and then raised arms and charged warstaves were pointed toward the tiny rise behind which Geoff and his band crouched. The gaily-coloured smoke given off by their warstaves was going to make concealing his position tricky, thought Geoff.

"Go," he said. By the time the first guardsmen charged over the crest of the rise, only scuffed earth and the stink of magic was there to greet them.

So it progressed as the afternoon faded into evening. Geoff and his band stung from the shadows of the trees and danced away into nothing before the magi could mount a response. Through it all, the column was led farther and farther to the east, and away from Market.

Geoff hunkered down in a raspberry bush that sprawled near a certain large and well-known dead tree. He had made good time from the last ambush, and knew that he might have to wait a little while for the others to arrive. He listened to the distant gurgle-rumble of the Hole, about a half-mile to the north of him, and thought about the next step.

He was still thinking when he heard a branch crack behind him. He spun, raised his warstaff, and barely avoided killing Aline, who was standing there looking sheepish and pained.

"Sorry Geoff," she growled through clenched teeth. "I made a mistake."

Geoff cocked his head – what was the girl talking about? His gaze skittered down Aline's arm and he saw. Aline's right hand was gone, and only shreds of sopping flesh showed at the end of her sleeve. The girl's mouth moved silently, and Geoff sprang to his feet. Without thought he tore the sleeve from his shirt and fastened a quick tourniquet to the young woman's arm – a desperate attempt to stop Aline's life from draining from her. He eased her to the ground and cradled her head in his arms.

"It just exploded in my hand. The warstaff." Aline's voice was quiet – almost a whisper. "I'm so sorry, Geoff."

"It wasn't your fault, Aline. Not at all. Nothing you could have done would have changed it." Was that true? Geoff didn't know, and it wasn't important at the moment.

"Oh," said Aline. "Good." The young woman – barely a woman at all – smiled in relief.

"Geoff? Aline? What's wrong?" A new voice cut through the evening silence. Micah stumped towards them on his short, powerful legs.

"Aline was hurt in the last ambush, Micah. I need you to get her to Will. Carry her if you have to, but get her there. Tell Will where we are, and that I'm going to keep hitting these magi all the way along the river to the bridge. Tell him we could use some help there. Micah… no matter *what*, Will needs to get that message."

Micah looked, for a moment, as if he might argue. Aline whimpered, however, and the young man subsided. Gently, he helped the injured girl gain her feet and the two figures were soon lost in the thickening gloom. Geoff settled in to wait for Jacob and Aline's brother Owyn.

Owyn, he thought, might be a problem. He and his sister were very close.

Owyn arrived about ten minutes later, Jacob Smithson following close on his heels. Evening was rapidly giving way to night, and soon there would be more moonlight than sunlight. Jacob plucked a few raspberries off of the bush under which Geoff had been hiding and munched on them ruminatively.

"You know—" he began. Owyn cut in before the thought could be developed.

"Where's Aline?"

Geoff looked at the young farmer and took a deep breath. He couldn't afford to lose Owyn to despair or frustration – couldn't afford to have him and Jacob questioning the safety of the warstaves. There are a hundred little lies upon which the future is built.

"I'm sorry, Owyn. One of the magi got her after the last ambush. She's hurt pretty badly, but Micah's taken her to Will. She'll be okay. You'll see her tomorrow, alright?"

Owyn and Jacob were oak-still. Owyn opened his mouth and closed it again. He blinked. Finally, he nodded once and sat down with his head in his hands.

Jacob swallowed a gob of raspberry and piped up.

"I thought that the magi put something on the little balls that stopped your heart if they cut you. Isn't that why they're so dangerous?"

If Geoff had had his way at that instant, Smithson's head would have burst into flames. For a moment he stood dumbfounded and then, unexpectedly, a response coalesced in some murky corner of his mind.

"I don't know. Maybe they wanted to take her alive." Geoff shrugged as casually as he could manage.

Jacob raised his eyebrows and whistled through his teeth.

"Bastards."

Owyn was making strange noises at their feet. Geoff glanced down in alarm, and was nearly bowled over as Owyn surged upward and sprinted off to the south, a pair of warstaves in his hands. A startled glance passed between Jacob and Geoff, and they charged after him.

Lonico

Stealth was abandoned completely in the mad run, and that may have been what saved them. The mage-led patrol they stumbled into certainly wasn't expecting their stealthy nemeses to come crashing through the undergrowth like donkeys. They must have been expecting to see another patrol of Lonicans – that was, at least, the only explanation Geoff could later come up with for their failure to immediately kill the three young valley men.

The mage and his three guards stood rooted to the spot as Owyn fell upon them. Snarling and cursing, the young farmer didn't even bother to discharge his warstaves. Instead he whirled them in great sweeping arcs that crushed heads, arms, and chests. The mage was down – dead – and Owyn was battering one of the guardsmen to his knees, before Geoff and Jacob even brought their weapons to bear.

Geoff quickly aimed his staff and killed one of the other guards, and beside him Jacob dropped the last. They watched in stunned silence as Owyn flailed at the kneeling guard. Eventually it was done, and Owyn turned to face them. He looked angry and embarrassed.

"Sorry," he said. "I—"

Geoff held up a hand and pointed at his ear. Owyn fell silent, but the night did not. Shouts and splintering branches echoed through the woods, the sounds emanating from the east, and the south, and the west. Geoff's tiny band was surrounded, or nearly so.

The three Laiians looked at each other for a long moment. Jacob opened his mouth to speak, and then clapped it shut again. He shrugged helplessly, eyes wide. Geoff cocked his head to the side, listening to the loudening sound of men crashing through the forest. For a moment he thought of Daniel – the innocent, unimpeachable 'hand whom Geoff had killed. Daniel, a man whose only fault had been a refusal to let the right thing go undone. Suddenly Geoff knew that it was time to make amends. He handed his warstaves to Jacob and Owyn.

"Take these," he said, wondering when he'd gotten so altruistic. "Get to Will. Don't fight unless you have no choice. I'll try to draw them off."

Jacob cocked an eyebrow. "How? At least take a staff."

Geoff thought of the orbs belted to his chest – and sighed. He removed two of the three and handed them to Smithson.

"Take these too. Try to figure out how they work if you can, but be very careful – they make the staves look like children's toys, and aren't… safe. Now go!"

Jacob frowned, but clapped Geoff on the shoulder.

"Good running, Geoff."

"You too, Smith. Owyn. Good luck."

Owyn nodded, finally out of his reverie, and the two men swept silently off into the dark. *They'll be fine*, Geoff thought. *I'm the one in trouble here.*

He jogged off to the north, taking care to step on as many dry leaves and fallen branches as he could, in order to keep the Lonicans' interest. The sounds of pursuit grew louder behind him. He was so intent on them that he lost his way, and burst from the bushes not at the slight narrowing of the river that had been his target but at the giant gurgling throat that was the Hole.

Geoff cursed fluently and lengthily as he turned to hurry west along the riverbank. He had only taken a few steps when he realized that his pursuers had reached the river and were moving towards him from that direction. He backed up and looked to the east, only to be confronted with the sheer blackness of the Rim, a scant hundred paces away. Suddenly the sound of crackling branches stopped, and Geoff turned to the south. A knot of magi and guardsmen had emerged from the woods and were looking at him curiously. One spoke.

"You'll lie facedown on the ground and submit to our justice or you'll be shredded where you stand."

Geoff slipped an orb from its sheath, thankful for the concealing darkness, and weighed his options. There weren't many. Surrender obviously wasn't one of them. Valatch would have him dead in an hour. He had swum the hole, in a manner of speaking, when he had convinced Will not to kill him. Now it looked like his only choice was to try it out for real.

In one motion he heaved the orb in the direction of the mage who'd spoken and launched himself backwards into the frigid water. He was vaguely aware of a great concussion and a ripple of screams behind him, but almost immediately his fight against the sucking current took all of his attention. His boots and clothing were not helping matters, he decided. Nor was the fact that he had been running all afternoon. It had been quite a day.

The northern shore looked very far away, indistinct in the night. A sudden tug of current snatched at his leg and Geoff felt the touch of panic. He thrashed wildly, a final frantic struggle against the water, but invisible arms of force swept him around in a great arc. The icy black water numbed his limbs, and fatigue stilled them. The growl of the Hole grew louder as he was sucked inexorably toward it, and within seconds it was the only sound in the world. The current strengthened further, to the point that Geoff's struggles against it were completely ineffective.

Suddenly the surface of the water curved away from him, and Geoff found himself staring directly down the swirling depths of the Hole. He screamed loud and long then. He could do nothing else. He circled the funnel once, twice, and then he fell into blackness. He swore he heard the damned thing chuckle as it sucked him down into the crushing black cold.

Oh well.

38

Yachem stared down at his feet. He was a bit worried about the right one. He was worried about the left one, too, of course, but mainly the right one. It was definitely worse than the left one. It had fewer toes, for one thing, and had taken on a distinctly angry colour, especially around some of the older wounds. He shifted gingerly on the stone floor, trying to make himself less comfortable. He found a position where his hip jabbed painfully into a pointed rock and leaned into it. He knew that the magi were spying on him – they had a series of mirrors that allowed them to keep a watch from… from wherever they spent their time when they weren't hurting him. They were watching and waiting. They wanted him to fall asleep. A few days ago they'd taken to bursting into the cell and performing their task whenever Yachem dozed off.

Yachem wasn't overly fond of their task, and he had decided not to give them the opportunity to practice it any more. He giggled a tiny bit. He'd been up for a long time now, and he knew that they must be getting frustrated. Probably they'd come in and hurt him soon even if he stayed awake, but maybe they'd let him sleep after. That might be nice. Maybe they'd just kill him. He wasn't sure if that would be nice or not, but he imagined that it might be restful.

Yachem watched the mildewed walls breathe for a little while, and a tiny voice inside his head suggested to him that he was probably crazy.

Oh well.

The pat-pat-pat of water slapping against basalt sounded through the cell, and Yachem heaved himself to his knees. He'd been trying to find the source of this water for days now, but the noise seemed to move around, to be always a little bit to his left. Water. The word sloshed around in his mind. Almost as much as he wanted sleep, he wanted water. A nice cool puddle of water – anything that he didn't have to lick from the ever-damp walls – would be wonderful. Pat-pat-pat.

Maybe if he just told them Ganarae's name, they'd let him go to sleep, or have some water. Or *both*. They were very curious about who he'd met at *The Mage's Staff*. Yachem had given them everything else, eventually. There was only so much that he was able to tolerate. He was sure that the few names he'd been given that evening so long ago were false – nobody was really named Magebane or Silktearer, at least not in *this* city – but Ganarae was a different story. Yachem had buried Ganarae's name in the deepest earth left in his mind. If he were to exhume it – well, the magi would probably kill him. Something to think about, definitely. Maybe tomorrow. Maybe after he'd found the source of the pat-pat-pats.

Pat-pat-pat. Yachem scuttled a little to the left and listened again. Pat-pat. To the left. Pat-pat-pat. Left again. The tiny stone cell that had become Yachem's world created confusing and contradictory echoes. Yachem pressed his ear against a wall. Nothing. The pat-pat-pat was gone. Maybe it was to the right? Yachem prowled back the way he had come, every ounce of concentration intent on his missing, teasing friend.

He had nearly completed his third circuit of the cell when he tumbled into sleep between one step and another. He didn't dream, and he wasn't immediately woken. Eventually a quiet but insistent noise intruded itself on his sleep – the rattling of an iron key in the stiff and balky lock to his cell. Long days of fear had trained him to recognize that sound, and fatigue fled like a gull before the storm.

Yachem staggered to his feet and attempted to ignore the angry shafts of pain that rode up his legs. He drew himself to his full height, and faced the door as it swung open. Chubby and Pretty entered. Yachem kept his composure with some difficulty. Chubby liked to work on Yachem's feet. He was responsible for at least one of the toes on the right one, and the gaping red wound on the sole of the left. Pretty's inclinations were still less pleasant. Yachem was glad that he'd found the will to stand, and all thought of betraying Ganarae left his mind. He wouldn't give these two the satisfaction. Maybe one of the kinder ones – the mage he called Happy only ever beat him with a switch, and even then Yachem could tell that his heart wasn't in it – but not these two. Chubby and Pretty were the worst.

Pretty leered at him, and all of a sudden Yachem decided that he'd had enough. The days or weeks or years of pain – however long it had been – were over. He'd die today. He carefully gauged the distance across the cell, drew back his head, and let fly a gob of spittle. It caught the dim torchlight and glowed like a spark as it arced across the tiny room and caught Pretty just to the left of his deeply pock-marked nose. Chubby gasped.

Pretty wiped the spew off of his face with a silk cloth – the tiny square of material worth enough to feed a family of servants for a year – and grinned at Yachem.

"We were going to kill you today, servant. For that, we're *really* going to take our time doing it."

Oops.

Chubby stepped to the side, and a large form materialized in the doorway. Yachem gaped at it, uncomprehending.

"Guard-sergeant," said Chubby, "bind this servant. Servant, you have five seconds to give us a name – a *real* name – or I swear you'll be days in dying."

Yachem was still staring with blank incomprehension at the guardsman advancing on him. A word escaped his lips before he could clamp them shut.

"Ga... Ganarae?"

There was a moment of absolute stillness in the tiny cell, and then things started to happen all at once. Pretty swore loudly and fumbled at the wand strapped to his belt, and Chubby raised his arm to destroy Ganarae, whose sword was already humming around in a tight arc toward him. There was a great spray of blood and Chubby collapsed to the floor. Yachem saw Ganarae stagger, clawing at gore covering his eyes, and Pretty brought his wand to bear.

Yachem never remembered crossing the cell. He never remembered battering the wand from Pretty's hand or slamming the mage's head back into the wall. He *always* remembered the sickening pop-crunch as he drove his thumb into Pretty's eye – hard – and the tone of the mage's scream as he died, and the warm wetness of his brains, and the smell as Pretty emptied his bowels, and the way he thrashed as his soul struggled to escape his body.

Eventually everything was still again, and Yachem felt a hand on his shoulder. He stood and faced Ganarae.

"If you need to kill me, I'll understand."

Ganarae had been smiling a sad little smile, but now the guard-sergeant just looked stunned.

"Kill you? Why would you think I'd do that?"

"I told them, Ganarae. I'm so sorry, but I told them everything."

The smile returned, a little.

"Oh? What did you tell them? Did you tell them anyone's names?"

"Well, I told them about Magebane and Staffsplitter and all the rest, and..." Yachem's voice trailed off as he thought.

"Nothing to worry about, then," said Ganarae. "You obviously didn't give them *my* name, and you didn't know anyone else's, so there's no need for any more talk about killing you."

Yachem looked down at his ruined body.

"Oh. Are you… are you sure? If you needed too…"

Ganarae's smile was gone again, but he still gripped Yachem by the shoulder.

"Yes Yachem. I'm sure. Can you walk?"

"I think so. For a bit." Yachem took a couple of experimental steps and nodded.

"Save your strength for when we need it, then. Hop on." Ganarae crouched, and Yachem clambered painfully onto his back.

The massive guardsman straightened and strode from the cell, moving as quickly and quietly as was possible. The two men took some sort of back passage to the outside world. Yachem was shocked to discover that it was late in the night. The sea fog was thick, and it was new moon dark. Nobody challenged the guard-sergeant with the unorthodox bundle as he trotted across the servants' bridge. Perhaps nobody noticed him.

Breathing in the salt-suffused air, Yachem began to be a little glad that he wasn't soon to be dead. It was, he thought, a start. The waiting city enfolded the two men in its anonymous darkness.

39

Jacob Smithson was sprawled on the cold ground, staring up into the sky and breathing heavily. Morning had finally come, and the sun was shouldering its way past the mountains in the east. Will coughed, quietly.

"And?"

"And so he told me and Owyn to get back to you, quietly, and that's what we did. I'm not sure where he went after that. Northeast, probably." Smith closed his eyes. "I heard something after we separated. Something loud. One of those, maybe." He waved a hand at the two orbs cradled in Will's hands. "He said to be careful with those, Will."

Will nodded.

"You told me already. I'll be careful. Why don't you rest for a while? I'll let you know when I need you. Okay?"

Smith only snored in response, and Will turned away. He threaded his way through the makeshift camp, nodding at frightened faces and flinty ones alike. Owyn, Aline and Micah were beside the river. Doctor Samuel's apprentice – he was the Doctor now, Will reminded himself – was hunched over Aline's prone form. He was muttering to himself. At a respectful distance, a crowd had formed.

Will's original group of twenty-five raiders had swelled now to at least a hundred men and women of all ages. They were armed with a motley assortment of hunting bows and long knives – some clutched noting more than heavy walking sticks. The few originals who held warstaves in their dirty and callused hands were grinning proudly. To a man and women these people were as hard as the roots of the trees, and seemed eager to do their part. They fell silent as Will approached.

He nodded briefly at them, and moved to the Doctor's side. The young man looked up and met his eyes. He shook his head slightly.

"She might make it, *maybe*, but her hand's gone."

Will nodded. Aline hadn't spoken since Micah had carried her into camp a few hours before. He put his hand on Owyn's shoulder and felt the young man stiffen. Owyn sought Will's eyes.

"I'll be okay, Will. She'll be okay. Right?"

Will could only nod. Hopefully they all would. Hopefully.

He turned and caught Micah's gaze. The stocky man moved toward him, exhaustion plain on his face.

"Will, we need to get moving. Geoff said he wanted to hit them at the river. He's all alone out there. He can't do it on his own."

Will shook his head slightly, and came to another hard decision.

"He's all alone out there indeed, Micah. Alone and unarmed, if he's even still alive. Geoff's not a stupid person. He's sometimes too clever for his own good, but, he's not going to throw himself at an army on his own. He'll hole up somewhere and wait for them to walk right past him. Anyway, we don't want to delay these magi any further. We *want* them to go bloody each other, slaughter each other, weaken each other."

Will privately doubted that Geoff had survived – he'd been in a very tight place from the sound of things – but he supposed that anything was possible. Geoff had had a knack for avoiding trouble since they were children.

"And then? When one of them wins? What do we do then?"

"Then we hit them as hard as we can. No city man is going to win this fight, Micah. Believe me. For now, though, get some sleep. We're going to be moving out this afternoon."

They spent the morning preparing, and the sun was sinking toward Citadel in the west before the little force began to filter away from their camp. In twos and threes they stole through the forest, grey and brown ghosts that drifted generally northeast by circuitous routes. Eventually, they would all congregate near the small clearing at the base of the path up to Bastion – the fortress where Valatch's forces were camped.

Will was among the first to arrive. He crept as close as he dared to the edge of the woods, and peered out. Samaranth's forces had made splendid time, and they had already begun to climb the narrow trail up the face of the cliffs.

Valatch's magi in Bastion had seen Samaranth's attempt to climb the narrow path to their redoubt. He'd turned some of his force, and they were pouring rocks – and worse – down onto the climbers. Samaranth's men were not fighting back, it seemed, but were holding massively thick shields above their heads and climbing upward. It was all very confusing, and Will was glad that he didn't have to think about it too much. Any of these magi would happily kill him and his people. They were all enemies of Laii, and if some of them turned on each other then so much the better. When he attacked he'd not leave a mage standing in the valley if he could help it – Valatch's or Samaranth's, it didn't matter.

Will spread his forces in a semicircle hugging the forest edge. The plan was simple. Wait for Samaranth's forces to gain the top of the mountain path. Hit them with arrows first, then warstaves. People armed with cudgels would finish the survivors. Right now, there was nothing to do but wait. The sun sank lower, picking out the viciously fought battle above in pink and orange light. At this distance the woomf and roar of warstaves discharging sounded like the gentle patter of rain on a wooden roof. It was quite pleasant, really.

There was a surge of movement at the top of the cliff, and the magic sluicing down the rock face slackened perceptibly. The magi at the bottom hurried forward and jostled for an opportunity to climb. Will nodded to Micah. The young man stood tall, sighted along the length of a broad-headed hunting arrow, and released the string. The arrow whistled jauntily as it cut through the air and, before it found its mark in the narrow shoulders of a yellow-clad mage, thirty more like it were in the air. The ragged flight of arrows had hardly landed in flesh and mail and earth before the rippling crack of warstaves echoed from the woods. Bodies collapsed, and the magi climbing up the cliff paused in shock. Another flight of arrows screamed through the chilly mountain air, and Will snatched up a fresh warstaff. Someone halfway up the cliff started screaming orders, and the magi began to climb with renewed vigour.

Will's raiders ran toward the carnage at the base of the path. Warstaves were picked up, and swords, and the dying were put down. Will had taken pains to instill the necessity of ruthlessness in his people. He hoped that – beyond the cadre of proven fighters – at least some of his people would be able to bring themselves to end a life or two. He hoped that *he* would, when it came to it. This wouldn't be at all like a fair fight. This would just be murder.

Will hurried to the base of the path with Jacob, Micah, and a hundred other vengeful souls at his heels. They didn't come under attack during the climb, except for a small rear-guard of guardsmen who were quickly dispatched by warstaves. Will supposed, as he scrambled and clambered upward, that everyone at the top of the cliff had more pressing concerns.

Lonico

Will crested the cliff and gaped at the whirling melee before him. Silk clad magi danced and spun between knots of struggling guardsmen. Gouts of smoke erupted from hands and wrists, and people – mage and guard alike – toppled by the dozen.

The noise was incredible. The ring-scrape of steel on steel, the crack and boom of warstaves and orbs and things that Will couldn't even recognize, punctuated a chorus of screams. Will had no idea how the magi or the guards could tell friend from foe. Nobody paid the swelling group of Laiians at the top of the path the slightest bit of attention, although some of the more rational magi had begun to withdraw down a narrow cleft between the mountains. Will watched, transfixed, as a tiny woman vaulted over a guard, managing in midflight to execute him with a flick of her hand and a *crack* of magic. She landed gracefully, spun on a toe, and was immediately cut down by another mage. The spell was suddenly broken.

Don't give them a fair fight. We'd never last. The tiny voice at the back of his mind galvanized Will into action.

"Staves up. Make every shot count. On my mark, end this invasion."

Will caught Jacob's eye and winked. The burly man nodded and dipped his hand into a leather pouch at his belt. Will did the same, waited three seconds, and raised a ceramic orb above his head. As he hurled it toward the staggering mass of combatants, he felt the concussion of forty warstaves being simultaneously fired. There were two great explosions of dirt and flame and shredded flesh – Smith's orb had also done its job – and then magi and their thugs began to fall like wheat.

"Keep attacking! Finish them!" Will's shout echoed through the jarring silence that followed that terrible moment. Men and women once again raised their warstaves and fired them in unison into the stunned magi. Before the Lonicans could locate the source of the attack, the valley men released another roaring barrage. Geoff had said that these city people thought the valley to be the home of monsters. It was surprisingly easy to live up to their expectations. All at once the magi were in full retreat, their internal conflict forgotten in the desperate struggle to survive a little longer.

The men and women of the valley surged toward the pass that cut between the mountains, Will in the lead. As they picked their way through the bodies crowding the narrow defile, however, Will stopped and peered downwards in surprise, turning a body slightly with one booted foot. A face had jogged at his memory. A prominent nose dominated a cadaverous face, bereft in death of the malignant energy that had suffused and animated it. Valatch looked like nothing more than an old man, now.

"Got him for you, Geoff."

Will pushed on, pausing not a moment to marvel at the ruined fortress of Bastion, or the ancient walls that had once lent a false sense of invincibility to the valley. The sounds of magical warfare echoed hollowly down the stone corridor, fainter and more sporadic with every second. By the time Will burst into the twilight world beyond the mountains, all was silent. He heard gasps from the Laiians as they took in the great panorama of dark forest, spread like a feast before them. He allowed himself a single glance and then turned his attention to the figures bunched on the far side of the bridge.

Will gestured for his men and women to take what cover they could find behind the low and wrecked walls of stone that crisscrossed the area. Cupping his hands around his mouth, Will bellowed across the canyon to the throng of magi and guardsmen.

"Magi. A word, please."

There was a moment of stillness, and then the human wall parted and two figures emerged, walking out into the middle of the bridge. Will heard nervous a shifting in the line of valley folk, and raised empty hands in a placating gesture. He took a few steps forward, but pointedly stopped far enough away from the two magi that they'd have trouble hitting him with their staves, should they prove untrustworthy.

From here he could see these two magi clearly. One was a tall woman, fine-featured, who was looking at Will as if he were an unusual specimen of flower. The other was a wizened little man whose eyes nevertheless burned with something like hatred. The man spoke, and his voice sounded like something rotten.

"What," he said, "do you want, Laiian?"

Will smiled and raised his arms.

"This valley is lost to you, mage, but your city may not yet be. Turn and leave this place, now and forever, or we'll destroy you where you stand." *You thought us monsters*, he thought, *and you've turned us into them.*

The silence stretched out for mere seconds, but with so many lives in the balance it felt like hours.

The female mage leaned in close to the male, and there was an exchange of words. The old man spun on his heels and stalked off across the bridge. The female watched him go for a moment, and then turned to regard the Laiians ranged before her. Eventually she spoke.

"Very well, Laiian. We shall withdraw. I hope that in the future—"

Will cut her off. "Wise decision, mage. Winter is coming, and your silks would have offered scant protection. Goodbye."

The mage opened and closed her mouth a few times, shrugged, and turned away. She strode back to her force, which immediately began to withdraw down the mountain road.

"Destroy the bridge," Will told Jacob. "We don't want them changing their minds. Oh, and if you can find him, ask Micah if he's willing to take some people and go hunting for the other entrance to the valley. We need to shut that one too."

Jacob grinned at Will and took off towards the milling band of valley men, axe and orbs in hand. Will barely heard the crunching booms as, a few minutes later, the bridge was reduced to kindling. He watched inky night fall over the trees of the forest, and then turned to walk back into Laii. There would be time to deal with the outside world in the spring. Right now, there was a harvest to bring in. With a rush of irritation, Will remembered that he'd never replaced the blade on his father's plough. He'd have to ask the smith about that.

Graham Angus

After

Yachem and Ganarae stood on the roof of *The Barking Seal* and watched the soft autumn sun set over the Rimwall. The columns of guardsmen – drawn into the city over the last week like a sharply intaken breath – were tapering away into nothing. Rumours had swirled through the city of magi for days. Rumours of battles in the mountains, and of the city's defeat at the hands of an ancient foe. The Laiians had bloodied the magi, and the city convulsed as it prepared for war. Rumours abounded too, albeit scarcely credited ones, of civil war among the magi, and of brother fighting brother in the western ranges.

The city throbbed and roiled, full to cracking with every guard that could be mustered. The magi, too, were busy. The lights of the great tower of the Council had been burning for weeks, and messengers galloped to and from the island at all hours. Vast gouts of smoke and steam issued from the spires on the island, and eerie lights burned in their windows. Street-corner prophets had appeared in impressive numbers, exhorting the citizens of Lonico to aid their protectors, join the guard, sacrifice, unite and obey. Such propaganda was proving to be quite effective. Some of the resistance movement's sympathizers had distanced themselves from the organization recently. There had been muttered suggestions that the resistance should be disbanded altogether, or at least postponed until the Laiian crisis was resolved. Ganarae was increasingly glum.

"We'll have the winter to prepare, I think." Yachem's voice broke the contemplative silence. Ganarae shot him a sideways look.

"Still with us then, Yachem?"

"Of course." Yachem flexed his knee experimentally and winced at the pain. "For what I'm worth." Ganarae smiled and turned his attention back to the sunset.

"Good." The silence grew again between the two men.

"I think," said Ganarae slowly, "you're right. There's no sense in trying anything now – the city's too full to walk down the streets, and people are scared enough as it is. We'll wait and see what the spring carries with it."

Yachem nodded and gazed toward the west. As the sun rolled down the low-sloping sky into the teeth of the mountains, his heart grew in his throat. Who'd have imagined, even a year ago, what would have become of his life? He'd never had such great goals – never so much to gain or so little to lose. Before him stretched the city, the watch bells just starting to toll their sunset dirge. He felt almost paternal towards it, he realized. He sniffed the wind, and the fish and salt smell of the sea mingled with the throat-catching odour of brewing magic and oiled metal.

"This spring will bring us war."

Ganarae looked at him again and shrugged.

"We can only hope."

Yachem nodded and hobbled toward the small door. The iron handle shrieked as he twisted the latch open and went inside.